Henry Cecil

A CHILD DIVIDED

HARPER & ROW, PUBLISHERS   NEW YORK

FIRST EDITION

LIBRARY OF CONGRESS CATALOG CARD NUMBER: 66–10642

M-P

Part One

erudite knowledge of charitable trusts and the doctrine of frustration does not necessarily make for good small talk at a party.

She hoped that Judge Bramcote would be different. Not that she really minded what he was like, so long as he did what she wanted.

And then she thought of those further visits to doctors. And all the unpleasant things that went with them, for her *and* her husband. She gave him full marks. He certainly showed the tolerance which the vicar had talked about. If she hadn't wanted a child, would she have submitted to all the unpleasantness for her husband's sake? She hoped she would. And then that awful morning when what they did could be described as a clinical performance, not actually under the eye of the doctor but the results of which were to be examined by him microscopically later.

Finally, the worst day of all when they proved that it couldn't be done. Bill had an obstruction which could not be removed, and the whole thing was off.

He took her away for a holiday after this, and they discussed adoption. Once again he fell in with her wishes. If she wanted a family, she should have one, even if other people had done all the work. Now there were different sorts of interviews. Not with doctors—except once, when their general health was inquired into and pronounced entirely satisfactory. Interviews with professional social workers, people anxious to see whether a child would have a good chance of happiness in such a home. Not an inquiry that can be answered as the result of a couple of visits.

People are on their best behavior when such inquiries are made. There can never be complete certainty about the prospective adopters unless those who make the inquiries go to live with them for a month or more. You can be on your best behavior all the time for a weekend, perhaps, but not for a month.

A number of unsuccessful marriages would never have taken place if the engaged couple had stayed at each other's homes for a month.

But, though it is not practicable for proposed adopters to be visited to this extent, all that could be done *was* done to find out if Mary and her husband would prove satisfactory adopters. Indeed, Mrs. Lyndhurst, the guardian appointed by the Court to safeguard the child's interests, was a particularly able and imaginative person and took the greatest care in carrying out her investigations.

"The wife," she wrote, in her confidential report to the judge, "is a charming young woman of thirty who will obviously make a most loving and kindly mother. It may be that she will be too loving and kindly, and the child may be somewhat spoiled. But there is no doubt that the child will enjoy the most loving care. I can only express the hope that he will always enjoy it. That is the only danger in this placement, the possibility that in his early days the child will be too much indulged and that later on he may resent or be irked by the warmth of his adopting mother's affection. As against that, I am personally a firm believer in *II Corinthians*, Chapter 13, and, though I do not claim to speak with the tongue of men or angels, I do believe that love never fails."

It is not altogether surprising that Mrs. Lyndhurst, with her somewhat unusual and individualistic reports, was popular with the judges to whom she reported, and none the less so because she was a particularly attractive woman.

About the husband Mrs. Lyndhurst wrote this:

"The husband, aged thirty-one, is a man who will always come second. He has done this literally in most of his activities. He nearly got a rugger blue; he got a blue for cricket, but lost it owing to his not being able to play in the varsity match; he got a second (a near-first) in his final examinations at Cambridge, and he will certainly come second to this baby if an adoption order is made. He is a thoroughly nice fellow (I apologize for the word 'nice' but I simply cannot find any other to convey what I mean), very fond of his wife, of absolute integrity, and he will be a kind and tolerant father. It is obvious to me that, while he is a willing party to this application, he has no burning desire to be a father, though I do not suggest for a moment that this is the reason that the applicants have so far not had children of their own. He wants this child solely because he knows how desperately his wife wants it. Apart from the unhappiness in which it would involve her, he would not be particularly depressed if an adoption order were refused. I am satisfied, however, that he will take a proper part in bringing up the child, and it may well be that, as the child takes on what from his point of view will be more human form, he may take a real interest in the boy. Especially if he turns out to be good at games. In some cases there would be a danger that, as Mr. Woodthorpe has been what I might call a successful failure, he would try to drive the boy into succeeding at all the things where he just failed. I do not think this will happen, the keynote of Mr. Woodthorpe's character being tolerance. I suspect that this is a home where even fools would be suffered gladly. They would be loved by Mrs. Woodthorpe and tolerated by her husband. I recommend that an adoption order be made."

Mary had never seen this report but she liked Mrs. Lyndhurst and had been very much encouraged by her. Over and over again, in the days while she was waiting for the application for adoption to be heard, she had reminded herself of the words that Mrs. Lyndhurst had used. She said them again to herself as she sipped her tea that night.

"Of course, it's for the judge, not me, to make the order," Mrs. Lyndhurst had said, "but I'm quite sure you'll have no difficulty in getting it, no difficulty at all."

But then she remembered with an icy feeling in her stomach that Mrs. Lyndhurst had added: "No difficulty at all—unless, of course, the mother withdraws her consent. But that's not at all likely." Not at all likely. That meant it was possible. The mother had signed the consent form apparently willingly enough. But she had the right to withdraw it. Why should she withdraw it? Why shouldn't she?

The fears of a prospective mother-by-adoption are different from but certainly no less than those of an ordinary prospective mother-for-the-first-time. In England, the chances of anything going wrong with an ordinary birth are small. Each year about one in five thousand mothers dies in childbirth or has a child who dies at birth. More than those that are struck and killed by lightning (only twelve a year) but still only very few. In all probability everything will be all right.

But when it comes to adoption, the mother can withdraw her consent at any time up to the making of the order. And, unless she does so capriciously or without thought for the welfare of the child, it will be given back to her, even though the prospective adopters have had the child for a year or more and will be heartbroken at losing it. It's not like a doll you can replace next day.

But the mother wouldn't withdraw her consent. She mustn't. Why should she put the child out for adoption if she wanted to keep it? Mary knew little about the mother, but the adoption society had told her all it knew. She was an educated girl, who said that she had met a solicitor at a dance, and a baby was the result. She did not even know the solicitor's name, or where he lived. She had no satisfactory means of keeping the child and she thought it would be in his interest to be adopted.

In fact, the girl had arrived unannounced at the adoption society's premises with the baby. She spoke of her proposal in such a matter-of-fact way to the representative who interviewed her that it caused that lady to say quite sharply:

"It's not like leaving a piece of baggage at a cloakroom, you know."

This had reduced the mother to tears. Eventually the formalities had been gone through, and the baby placed with the Woodthorpes.

What a day that was. Mary remembered it so vividly. At last it had happened. At last. She didn't think then of the problems or pitfalls of Adoption Law. She had her baby. She had had to wait so long. Her joy was as much as a real mother's. And she had the advantage of being up and about at the time. No stitches had to be removed in her case. And she loved it from the start. Just like a real mother. The small thing that was to be hers.

Her husband was not in the least jealous. He loved to see Mary happy. In a way, she was his child as well as his wife. And to watch her eyes shine with happiness for whatever reason was the greatest pleasure for him. The shining eyes of a woman in love, whether with a man or a baby, are among the sights of the world. To rank with great sunsets. And, like sunsets, they are seldom satisfactorily reproduced artificially. A notable exception was provided by Mary Astor at the end of the film of *Dodsworth*.

Mary's eyes certainly shone now. She had her husband and her baby. Could any happiness be more complete? After the first wonderful month, when the baby most considerately suffered from nothing at all, she realized that happiness could be more complete. The baby wasn't yet hers. But it was. It must be. Another two months and it would be. But at any time within the three months the mother could ask for her piece of baggage

back again. Mrs. Lyndhurst assured Mary that there was no
sign whatever of the mother appearing to have changed her
mind. And then came the great day when the mother yet again
stated that she wanted the order made.

Mary thought gratefully of the moment when Mrs. Lyndhurst
gave her that news over the telephone. But later the same day
she had been told something that at the time disturbed her.
She had been advised by a lawyer friend to have a solicitor to
represent them. Both she and her husband asked why this
should be necessary in a straightforward case. "You never
know," their friend had said. "There are technicalities in these
matters, and it's as well to have a lawyer to keep you straight."

Although she was a little worried at the idea of having to go
to a lawyer, she had become most grateful in the end for the
advice. They had gone to see a Mr. Luttrell, who was recom-
mended to them as having great experience in adoption cases.
She remembered his first words after they'd been introduced.

"Adoption, is it? If I'd got one, you could have that."

"I beg your pardon?"

"Children are the devil. Horrible to think I was one myself
once. And no better than the others. Probably worse. Lucky
there are people like you in the world. With girls dropping
children all over the place. Wasn't so fifty years ago. People
minded then. Nobody cares what you do today. Illegitimate, I
suppose?"

"Yes."

Mary's husband could not resist adding that the father was a
solicitor.

"A solicitor, eh? Not in my firm, I hope. What's his name?"

"They don't know."

"Oh, come, this won't do. Of course they know."

"They say they don't."

"Which Court is this in?"

They told him.

"This is serious," he said. "Tell me all you know about the mother and her solicitor."

Mary remembered her sudden fear. Mrs. Lyndhurst had said everything would be all right. And now this lawyer was saying it was serious. What was serious? Mr. Luttrell told her.

"Now, some judges take the view that the father of a bastard doesn't count. Quite right. He shouldn't. He's had his bit of fun. And that should be that. Now, it's true his consent isn't necessary, but if—and only if—he's liable to contribute to the maintenance of the child either under an agreement or an affiliation order he is by law entitled to be heard by the Court as to whether an adoption order should be made."

"Yes, I was told that," Mary's husband had said, "but this man didn't even know there was a child. He couldn't have become liable to pay for it. The mother doesn't even know who he is."

"Quite right," said Mr. Luttrell. "So the mother says."

"I don't understand."

"If what the mother says is true, all well and good. But suppose it isn't?"

"But how can we tell?"

"You can't, without the mother being questioned a good deal more. And probably she is telling the truth. But there are cases where mothers have special reasons for not telling the truth."

"Why should this be one?"

"Why indeed?"

"Then what is serious?"

"One of the judges at this Court is very difficult about these cases."

"In what way?"

"He won't just accept the mother's say-so in cases like this."

"What does he do then? Refuse the adoption order?"

"Oh gracious, no. He just insists on her being more closely questioned. Sometimes even has her summoned before him so that he can ask the questions. I must admit that he does sometimes get results. Finds people whose addresses he has been assured nobody knows."

"But how does that hurt us?"

"Well, for one thing, it delays the making of an order; for another, it causes everyone a lot of inconvenience; but, worse than anything, while all this is going on, the mother may change her mind and ask for the child back. Indeed, I knew of a case where this happened. The mother was so fed up at being questioned by the judge that she suddenly said she wouldn't answer any more questions and she'd trouble the judge to hand her back the baby."

"How terrible."

"Indeed it was, and might have been worse."

"Worse?"

"Yes—he might have handed it back. Fortunately, in that case I was able to satisfy the old fool that the mother was being unreasonable, and so my clients got the child in the end. But it was touch and go."

"What are we to do, then?"

"You? Nothing. There are two judges at this particular Court. The judge who makes the difficulties is called Hazlewell. I shall now find out whether your application is coming before him."

"And if it is?"

"Quite simple. I shall try to get the case adjourned to a day when it will come before the other judge, Judge Bramcote."

"What's he like?"

"A judge after my own heart. A most reasonable man. He doesn't worry about putative fathers—which, by the way, is what gentlemen who behave like your solicitor friend are called."

"Suppose you can't get the case taken by him?"

"I can only try," said Mr. Luttrell. "But I can try very hard, if necessary."

Whether or not Mr. Luttrell had had to try very hard, he succeeded. The case was to be heard before Judge Bramcote. But, even so, Mary got little sleep herself though she looked at Hugh still sleeping peacefully in his crib and she looked at her husband who was sleeping just as peacefully. Tomorrow she would be taking Hugh to Court to make him hers. She smiled. And Bill's too, of course, she suddenly thought.

2 Change of Judges

THE DAY BEFORE THE CASE WAS DUE TO BE HEARD,
Bill Woodthorpe was chatting about it to a friend.

"What do you have to do?" asked the friend. "Go before a
judge and take the adoption vows or whatever they are?"

"I don't know about any vows. We certainly have to go before a judge."

"I expect you have to swear something or other. These lawyers are fond of oaths. Don't see much point in them myself,
the way some people take them. I was on a jury once. Policeman gabbled it off as though it meant nothing. The prisoner
was very different. He held the Bible right up and said it very
slow and very loud. Odd thing was, the policeman told the
truth and the prisoner lied like blazes."

"Nobody's told us we'll have to swear anything. And we've
been to a solicitor."

"Well, he should know."

"We didn't ask him, as a matter of fact."

"I expect he'd have told you. All the same, I don't see why you shouldn't make some sort of promise to bring the child up as if it were your own."

"But people wouldn't adopt children unless that's what they intended."

"Same applies to getting married. Most people even today, I suppose, don't get married unless they intend to stay married. Forsaking all others and all that. But they take their vows just the same."

"Not in a registry office."

"Don't they make any promises there?"

"I wouldn't know for certain, but I don't think so."

"Well, you'll soon know in your case. Hope it'll go all right."

"Thanks. We've had a bit of luck, as a matter of fact. We've changed judges. There are two judges in the Court we're going to. Our solicitor told us that one was technical and made difficulties. So he's got our case before the other."

"Can you choose them like taxis?"

"Don't ask me. Our solicitor just said he'd change them if he could. And he did. Ours not to reason how."

The change had, in fact, been effected quite simply. Mr. Luttrell had gone to the Court and issued two applications in other cases in which he was concerned. He had asked for a date when Judge Bramcote was sitting. There was no difficulty in obtaining this. He then went before Judge Hazlewell.

"Your Honor," he said, "I have two applications before Judge Bramcote on the thirteenth. I also have an adoption matter before Your Honor on the twelfth. It would be a great convenience if all these cases could be heard on the same day. I wonder if Your Honor would be prepared to adjourn the adoption case to Judge Bramcote's list."

"Will it take long?" asked the judge.

"No, Your Honor," said Mr. Luttrell and added incautiously, "only a few minutes."

"Only a few minutes for an adoption case?" queried the judge somewhat severely. "You seem to treat it like the sale of a motorcar. Will it be on hire-purchase by any chance?"

Mr. Luttrell forced a smile.

"Forgive me, Your Honor. Your Honor is perfectly right to reprove me. What I should have said is that there is no opposition from the mother and the guardian has made a favorable report."

"And what about the father? Does he consent too?"

"He's a putative father, Your Honor, and his consent is not necessary."

"Has he been served?"

"He has never contributed to the maintenance of the infant, Your Honor."

"Has he been served, Mr. Luttrell?"

"He's not entitled to be served, Your Honor."

"I wish you could answer a direct question directly, Mr. Luttrell. Has he been served?"

"No, Your Honor. We don't even know where he is."

"Have you tried to find out?"

"The mother says it was a casual acquaintance."

"A lot of them say that to cover someone else."

"We have no reason to believe this is the case here, Your Honor."

"What steps—" began the judge, and then stopped. "What it really comes to is that you'd prefer Judge Bramcote to deal with the matter."

"I have two other applications before the learned judge," said Mr. Luttrell.

"I would have been more favorably impressed with your application, Mr. Luttrell," said the judge, "if you'd just said you want my learned brother to hear this case. I should certainly have acceded to such an application. Personally, I think it would be an excellent thing if, where possible, people were allowed to choose their judges. What better tribunal can parties have than the one they ask for? Of course, if they can't agree on a judge, that's another matter. But in your case there's no opposition to the application, so you shall certainly have Judge Bramcote to deal with it. I only wish you'd left out the trimmings."

"It's very difficult for advocates," said Mr. Luttrell. "The late Mr. Justice Swift said that one should wrap things up."

"No doubt that's how he liked it. I should have thought that by now, Mr. Luttrell, you would have known that I don't. But you shall still have Judge Bramcote. But just one word of warning to you. One day an unknown, unserved putative father may make trouble."

"I'm much obliged to Your Honor," Mr. Luttrell said, and was more than ever thankful from his clients' point of view that his application had been granted.

Bill and Mary knew none of the details. They were quickly given the good news that the warmhearted nontechnical Judge Bramcote was to hear the case.

"They say the judge we've got is a very nice fellow. I'm quite looking forward to it, as a matter of fact. Never been in Court before. Of course, this isn't actually in Court. Adoption cases are always heard privately in the judge's room."

"What'll you do to celebrate? Take her out somewhere?"

"Out? With Hugh at home? Our going-out days are over for the moment."

"Baby sitters?"

"Don't you believe it," said Bill. "I dare say that in time

we'll get round to it. But for the moment she'll be the only baby sitter in our house in the normal way. I suppose she might use me when it's absolutely necessary. But she won't trust anyone else with Hugh at present. I shall have to get a TV set or a book or something."

3 The Day

"SLEEP WELL, DARLING?" MARY ASKED BILL THE
next morning.

"Wonderful. And you?"

She did not answer and he did not ask her again.

"What shall I wear?" she asked. "The green with the straw
hat?"

"That would be fine."

"Or the blue, do you think? With the same hat."

"You look lovely in that."

"Then you prefer it to the green?"

"I wouldn't say I preferred it."

"You mean you like the blue better?"

"I think they're both nice."

"Nice? You mean you don't like either. What about my new
suit? Or will it be too hot?"

"It might be a little warm."

"But I won't want a coat."

"There is that."

"Do you really like the suit? You've never said much about it."

"It's charming."

"Not just nice."

"Very nice."

"Would you like it better than the green or the blue?"

"Not better. As well."

"Then you don't like any of them."

"Of course I like them."

"But you distinctly said you didn't."

"I didn't, really."

"You said they were nice, didn't you? Do you know a worse word to throw at a girl?"

"I meant it nicely. Oh dear, there I am again. No, really, darling, I love all your dresses."

"No discrimination?"

"None at all," he said firmly, "when you're in them. I only see you. I don't notice the clothes."

"Other people do. You wouldn't like me not to look nice, would you?"

"Nice?" he queried.

They both laughed.

"I shall wear black," she said, "with a white hat. That'll fetch him."

"Wonderful idea."

"Or white with a black hat?"

"Either."

"Which?"

"Well," he considered, "on the whole, black with a white hat."

"Then you think I'm too fat to wear white?"

"I never even hinted at it."

"Then why did you say black with white?"

"I meant to say one or the other."

"Then you just said anything. You tossed up for it. That's not much help to me."

"You know perfectly well," said Bill, "that whatever I say, you'll wear what *you* decide."

"You may be surprised to know that I take a lot of notice of what you say."

"Not about your clothes."

"Perhaps you're right. Anyway, tell me how I look."

She tried first one dress and then another, and then a third and fourth and back to the first again. At this stage Bill suggested that they might have breakfast first or they'd be late. The word "late" had an electrifying effect on Mary. She put on a black frock and got out a white hat.

"That's settled," she said.

But later, when Judge Bramcote actually saw her, she was in green.

They arrived early at the Court and had to wait an agonizing quarter of an hour before Mrs. Lyndhurst arrived. But there was still no Mr. Luttrell.

"How are you?" said Mrs. Lyndhurst warmly. "Sleep well?"

"So-so," said Mary.

"That's better than most of them," said Mrs. Lyndhurst. "If it were my turn I wouldn't sleep at all. You slept like a top, I expect, Mr. Woodthorpe."

"Splendid, thank you."

"They always do," said Mrs. Lyndhurst. "Just the reverse of the other thing. I slept beautifully the night before my first baby, but my husband was a wreck. With adoptions it's the other way round. Well, I'm glad you've nothing to worry about. Lucky we've got Judge Bramcote."

"I'm so relieved," said Mary.

"And well you might be," said Mrs. Lyndhurst. "Judge Hazlewell's a good enough judge in his own way. But he's so persnickety. Ten to one he'd have adjourned this case for at least a month."

"I couldn't have borne it," said Mary.

"Well, you'd have had to," said Mrs. Lyndhurst, "like the others. Ah, here's the man who's saved you from that dreadful fate."

Mr. Luttrell had arrived. He shook hands with all of them.

"I'm afraid I've a slight disappointment for you," he began, and then, as he saw Mary's color change, hastily said: "Oh— it's nothing to worry about. But I'm afraid the judge can't take your case first. He's in the middle of trying a case where one of the barristers has to get away to the High Court. And he's promised to finish it before he does yours. That's all. I don't suppose he'll be very long."

Mary was so relieved that it was nothing worse that her disappointment at having to wait was much less than it would otherwise have been.

"Give you a chance to see the old boy in Court first," went on Mr. Luttrell. "It's all experience. You may want to send your boy to the Bar. Funny if you did. Or a solicitor even. We're the lower branch, you know. Very humble. But between you and me I don't know what we've got to be humble about. Our exams are harder and cover much wider ground. We usually spend five years in getting qualified, while a barrister spends only three. And, more important than that, we know something about the job before we're qualified, while a barrister knows nothing. He learns it afterward. But the law's a funny thing."

They went into Court and after a short time Judge Bramcote came in.

"Be uncovered in Court," said the elderly usher as everyone

1 The Night Before

MARY WOODTHORPE DID NOT THINK THAT SHE slept at all during the night before she and Hugh were to appear before Judge Bramcote. Of course, she had slept part of the time. People who "haven't slept a wink all night" have probably had, if not enjoyed, at least half their normal sleep. Mary certainly had less than this. Between two and three in the morning she made herself a cup of tea, while Hugh lay sleeping peacefully. She tried to read, but unsuccessfully. She tried more successfully to think the night away. To think of everything that had gone before.

Her wedding, white and happy; even what the vicar said: "Two things you need for a happy, lasting marriage. You have the one—love. Have you the other—tolerance?" Her honeymoon. Glorious. So glorious that she was even happy when it was over, eager to start this new life together.

And then the happy years, happy for him in everything; for her, too, in the beginning, but later with her happiness sadly

qualified, as the months and years went by with never even a
hint of a family being on the way. Well, perhaps a hint from
time to time, a hint which made things worse because it was
always belied.

She remembered when, a little shyly, a little embarrassed,
she first mentioned the matter to her husband. They loved each
other dearly, but he had no particular longing for a child. Because he loved her and knew she wanted one, he would have
been happy to have one for her sake. But he had to admit that
selfishly he realized that, once the family started, he could not
receive all Mary's attention. So while, to please Mary, he hoped
for children, he bore their absence quite cheerfully.

All the same, when Mary mentioned the matter and wanted
to seek help, he agreed to all her suggestions. She remembered
this gratefully, because she knew well enough that he did not
share her deep and dreadful longing, dreadful because it might
never be satisfied.

How many years was it? Three before they went to a doctor.
And then another year with temperature charts meticulously
kept by her. She didn't mind his teasing her about them, nor his
somewhat coarser jibes when her temperature rose above normal. Once it was just flu.

And then more visits to the doctor, and those two days in the
hospital. This must do it, she had told herself. How she had
prayed the night before. And the thought of her prayers then
made her pray now for a successful meeting with Judge Bramcote. And then the remembrance that her operation had made
no difference made her fearful that Judge Bramcote might have
no more effect on her life than the surgeon. She had met plenty
of doctors before. But no judges—oh, yes, she had. Once. For a
few minutes at a party. Mr. Justice Richmond. From her point
of view a dull, lugubrious man, though the life and soul of the
party when intricate legal problems were discussed. But an

stood up. No one took his hat off for the very good reason
that he'd have been told to take it off pretty smartly if he had
come into Court with it on, even if the judge wasn't sitting.
The judge bowed to counsel and sat down. Everyone else followed suit.

"Clarke against Evans, part heard," said the clerk, and the
judge closed his eyes.

Judge Bramcote had at one time had a slight affection of the
eyelids which made it more comfortable for him sometimes to
keep his eyes closed. He remained fully awake but it was a little
disconcerting for witnesses or advocates who were not aware
of his habit. Once a boy of seventeen was in the witness box
and he suddenly noticed that the judge was apparently asleep.
It so happened that the witness box was very close to the advocate who was questioning him.

"Where were you at ten-thirty on the night of the thirty-
first of October?" he was asked.

"Having a bit of shut-eye," said the boy, and then very
boldly added in a stage whisper, "like him."

A stage whisper is intended to be heard, but the boy had
certainly not intended the judge to hear it.

"What did you say?" said the judge, apparently still asleep.
The boy was dumb.

"I didn't get the last part of that answer," repeated the judge.
"The witness dropped his voice."

The judge opened his eyes and looked at the boy.

"I quite understand," he said, "that you find it difficult to
give evidence. I don't suppose you've been in a Court before
and you probably feel nervous. We all understand that. But
you must try to speak up. Otherwise, I shall be continually asking you to do so and that will make you more nervous than
ever. Now, I've got down: 'At ten-thirty I was having a bit of
shut-eye.' What did you say after that?"

This was the first time this boy had ever taken an oath and he knew that to tell lies in the witness box was a serious matter. If you were found out, that is. And he knew that several people, at least, must have heard what he said. He looked round despairingly for help. The judge noticed his apparent terror.

"I know you feel nervous," he said in kindly tones, "but there's no need to upset yourself unduly. No one is going to be unkind to you or shout at you or anything like that. That sort of thing is reserved for the films—and possibly other countries. No one bullies witnesses in this country, certainly not in this Court. Now come along, just repeat what you said after"—the judge looked down at his notebook—"after 'shut-eye.' "

The boy gulped.

" 'Like him,' " he whispered.

" 'Like him'?" repeated the judge and wrote it down. "And who was 'him'?" he asked, and added: "But do please keep your voice up. I only just heard what you said. Try to speak as loud as I do. Say 'like him.' "

Again the boy whispered it.

"Come, you must do better than that," said the judge. "You said the first part quite well. What was it?"

He looked at his notes again and repeated, " 'At ten-thirty I was having a bit of shut-eye.' Now, you say that, and add 'like him' at the end."

Almost in despair the boy said loudly:

"At ten-thirty I was having a bit of shut-eye like—" and then his voice failed and the "him" was in a whisper.

"That's much better," said the judge, "except for the last word. Now, let's get on. What was I asking you? I've forgotten."

Normally counsel would have prompted the judge, but for once no one did.

"Mr. Lancaster, can you help me? What was I asking the witness?"

"I'm afraid I've forgotten too," said counsel, telling a lie which would have brought him no rebuke from the Benchers of his Inn.

"Oh well," said the judge, "if it was important I'll remember it later," and the incident closed. But from that time Judge Bramcote was familiarly known as "Old Shut-eye."

Mary had been told of his nickname, but not of the story which gave rise to it.

"When the Court rose," said counsel, "I had just completed my submission on the issue of estoppel. I now come to Central Property and High Trees."

The judge opened his eyes, which he still closed sometimes from habit.

"Are you going to rely on High Trees?" he asked.

"Yes, Your Honor."

"What time do you want to be in the High Court?"

"Immediately after lunch, Your Honor."

"Well, if you're really relying on High Trees, you won't get there. A full argument on that subject will take, I should think—" the judge paused and thought for a moment. "It will take," he went on, "about four days."

Counsel looked at each other, and the judge closed his eyes.

"Well, what do you want to do about it?" he asked.

There was a whispered conversation between counsel. Then one of them spoke.

"Perhaps, if Your Honor would give us a few minutes, we will be able to resolve the difficulty."

"Certainly," said the judge. "I've an adoption case to hear and I'll take it now while you discuss the matter."

The judge rose and went to his room.

"That's the third time I've seen that happen," said Mr. Luttrell. "You're in luck. There's a lot of controversy about this case of High Trees. Whenever anyone raises it here, the judge says it'll take four days to argue and off they go and settle the case."

"But why?" asked Bill.

"Why? Expense," replied Mr. Luttrell. "Four days here, eight in the Court of Appeal and a dozen in the House of Lords. And all over six and eightpence."

"Six and eightpence!" said Bill incredulously.

"Not literally," said Mr. Luttrell. "But, when you think of what the cost of all these hearings is going to be, it'll have to be a pretty large sum in dispute to make it worth while. A couple of hundred pounds would be made to look pretty silly."

"Well, I'm very grateful to those trees," said Mary. "May they grow higher and higher."

A few minutes later they were shown into the judge's room. He still had his gown on but had removed his wig. He greeted them most affably and glanced admiringly first at Mrs. Lynd-hurst and then at Mary.

"Come along in and sit down. I'm glad to say your case isn't going to take four days."

"I'm glad to hear that too, Your Honor," said Mary.

"I bet you are," said the judge. "Don't suppose you slept much last night."

"I didn't sleep a wink, as a matter of fact," said Mary, start-ing to love this judge—not, of course, as much as Hugh and Bill but momentarily very much indeed.

"Well, I'm pleased to say," went on the judge, "that there are no complications in your case. All the hard work's been done already." He again looked admiringly at Mrs. Lyndhurst.

"Some people begin to think that adoption's little more than a formality. But it isn't, you know. It's very serious. But, as I glass of sherry. He was a new vicar and this certainly made a good impression on all concerned.

Among the godparents chosen by Mary and Bill had been a rich adopted uncle called Sir Nicholas Bent. He was a man who preferred giving orders to receiving them and it was easy to offend him.

The vicar handed round the sherry and allowed a certain amount of small talk before he disclosed the real reason for his invitation.

"A very good baby," he said. "I don't suppose you remember whether *you* were, Sir Nicholas?"

"I can't say that I do. But I once saw a man who said he had even earlier recollections."

They were incredulous and asked for details.

"I was in India at the time," said Sir Nicholas, "and happened to wander into the High Court in Bombay. A young man was in the witness box. His actual age was of paramount importance in the case. I suppose he was alleging infancy or something of the sort. 'When were you born?' asked counsel. 'On the twentieth of November, 1914,' said the young man. 'But you can't know that yourself,' said the judge. 'You only know what you've been told.' 'I know I was born on the twentieth of November, 1914,' persisted the young man. 'You actually remember being born, do you?' asked counsel. 'Certainly.' 'Did it hurt?' asked the judge. 'Not particularly,' replied the young man. I enjoyed that 'not particularly,' " said Sir Nicholas.

"Well, I can't cap that," said the vicar, "but I certainly remember being christened."

"Not really?"

"Yes, really. It was only ten years ago. I'm a comparative latecomer in the Church. That's why I've asked you to come and have a chat after the service. I hope you don't mind. Another glass of sherry?"

·

said, by the time a case gets to me all the work's been done. I know all about your previous convictions and that sort of thing."

He smiled.

"I'm quite sure that the child couldn't go to a better home. I know Mrs. Lyndhurst agrees, because she's already said so. Not changed your mind, Mrs. Lyndhurst?"

"No indeed, Your Honor."

"And I suppose you haven't either?" asked the judge, looking first at Mary and then at Bill. "Just as well to know before we tie the little fellow up for life. Good little chap. I saw him in Court. Not a word. Some of them scream the house down."

"No, we haven't changed our minds," said Mary and her eyes shone like Mary Astor's.

"Well, that's good," said the judge, "for I'm sure the young man would have been most disappointed. What's he going to be, I wonder. His father's a solicitor, I gather. I hope he takes more care with his clients. You're an accountant, Mr. Woodthorpe," he went on. "Well, you can't go wrong in that profession these days. You govern the world pretty well. And I'm glad to see you're a cricketer. I don't suppose Mrs. Woodthorpe's much interested."

"No, Your Honor."

"My wife isn't either. But that won't worry either of you now. The boy's name is Hugh. D'you want to keep Hugh? Or to add any other names?"

"We'd just like Hugh, Your Honor."

"Well, one name's enough for anyone, unless your surname is Smith or Jones or something. Then you need half-a-dozen. The child's not been christened yet, I gather. Have you made arrangements with the vicar?"

"Yes, Your Honor," said Mary, "but we wanted to wait till he was really ours."

"I know," said the judge. "Most people do. But, if you honestly believe in baptism, surely it should be done as soon as possible?"

"But godparents, Your Honor?" queried Bill. And Mary could have hit him. Why put a spoke in the wheel at this stage? It was all going so beautifully. But she need not have worried.

"Yes, there is that," said the judge. "If for some reason an adoption order were refused and the child went back to the mother, and you'd got Uncle Arthur and a couple of friends as godparents, it might be rather awkward. How could they discharge their duties as godparents? So perhaps you're right. Now, Mrs. Lyndhurst, is there anything you want to add to your report?"

"No, thank you, Your Honor."

"Good," said the judge. "Well, I shall make the order with very much pleasure, and I hope you will all be very happy. But I also hope the young man isn't as good as this all his life. It wouldn't be natural."

The judge stood up and shook hands with Mary and Bill and they went out, Mary's eyes shining with a wholesome mixture of love and tears. Suddenly they heard a voice.

"Remember me?" said Mr. Luttrell. He had done nothing before the judge except bow and smile, but he had earned his fee when he arranged for Judge Bramcote to hear the case.

"I'm so sorry," said Mary and Bill together. "We can't thank you enough," went on Mary. "What a wonderful judge. I can't tell you how happy you've made us."

"Fine," said Mr. Luttrell. "It wouldn't have been like that before Judge Hazlewell."

Mr. Luttrell was right. It would not have been the same before Judge Hazlewell. And, had he tried the case, the history of Mary and Bill might have been very different.

4 *Godfathers*

"HATH THIS CHILD BEEN ALREADY BAPTIZED OR no?" asked the vicar. There was no reply. This is quite normal. Presumably the reason why the question is seldom answered is because the parents leave it to the godparents and vice versa. Of course, in the ordinary case the only people who can know are the parents. A godparent could only truthfully answer, "Not as far as I know," or "To the best of my knowledge and belief, no." Answers which would take most vicars a little by surprise. But usually no one says anything and for once silence is treated as a negative answer. Sometimes the vicar himself says, "No?"

When Hugh was christened, no one could truthfully have answered the question, but this was not the reason for no one's answering. The vicar said, "No?" and proceeded with the service. In fact, the vicar was right. Hugh had been known as Hugh but not christened. After the service was over the vicar invited Mary and Bill and the godparents to the vicarage for a

"No, thank you, vicar," said Sir Nicholas, and they all followed suit.

"Now, please sit down," said the vicar. "The trouble with converts," he went on, "is that they're too enthusiastic. I'm afraid I'm a good example."

"From what were you converted, may I ask?" said Sir Nicholas. "Not Buddhism, by any chance?"

"No indeed. From nothing. That was a great advantage. I had nothing to unlearn. No prejudices, no beliefs. A clean slate. Wonderful start. Same as this baby. That's where you come in, Sir Nicholas, and the other godparents. It's a heavy responsibility."

Sir Nicholas Bent, aged sixty-four, chairman of his local justices, one-time M.P., retired from the army with the rank of brigadier, was beginning to regret taking on the job. He was not going to be cross-examined by a thirty-five-year-old vicar, even if he was an enthusiastic converted Christian.

"I'm afraid I shan't be able to stay very long," he began.

"I won't keep you any longer than I have to," said the vicar, "but I feel sure that a man of your age and, may I say, distinction will be only too pleased to hear what I expect from my godparents."

"Your godparents?"

"Godparents of children I christen. I feel a responsibility toward you similar to that which you should feel toward the child. Are you sure you won't have that glass of sherry?"

Sir Nicholas took a swift look round at his friends. This time he gave the signal to accept.

"Cheers," said the vicar. "Now, first of all," he went on, "a few words about the devil and all his works. Sir Nicholas, as by far the oldest of you, must know more about them than the lot of us put together."

"I am not yet in my dotage," said Sir Nicholas, who was

irked by this repeated reference to his age. In fact, he was sensitive on the subject and did not give his birthday in *Who's Who*.

"You're not a year more than sixty-seven," said the vicar. "I'll warrant that."

"You're quite right," said Sir Nicholas, "I'm sixty-four."

"I don't suppose you'll look much older than you do already when you're sixty-seven. Even when you're seventy," he added.

"You mean I look seventy, do you?" asked Sir Nicholas with some asperity.

"A young and healthy seventy," said the vicar. "As a matter of fact, I thought that *was* your age. I said sixty-seven because I always knock off two or three years to please people. That's one of the permissible lies. At least, I think so. Now, for the devil and all his works. Have you had great difficulty in resisting him, Sir Nicholas? Indeed, have you resisted him at all?"

Sir Nicholas remained fiercely silent.

"Come along, Sir Nicholas. We're all friends, and Hugh won't be able to take it in yet. Unless he's like your Indian witness."

"Vicar," said Sir Nicholas, "I have lived the normal life of a respectable man and I don't propose to be cross-examined about it."

"The sin of pride," said the vicar, "is not by any means the worst, I assure you, but I hope you will do your best to see that this child does not suffer from it. Too often I find that godparents think their duties are limited to taking part in the baptism service and remembering a few birthdays and Christmases. That isn't it at all, you know. The religious instruction of this child is committed to your care, no doubt in concert with the parents, but it is still primarily your responsibility."

"What a lovely word—'parents,' " said Mary. Then she added: "I'm sure Uncle Nicholas will make a wonderful godfather, Vicar."

"There's no need to put in a plea for me, Mary," said Sir Nicholas. "I'm quite capable of defending myself."

"Defending?" said the vicar. "No one's attacking you, I assure you, Sir Nicholas; it is only because you are the oldest. Everything I have said applies equally to the other godparents."

"That they'll look the same as they do now when they're seventy?" asked Sir Nicholas.

The vicar laughed.

"You do worry about your age, don't you, Sir Nicholas," he said. "I can't think why. There are lots of people older than you. You're still in the coronary-thrombosis bracket, I may tell you. No one's old till he's past that point, whatever age he may look."

Sir Nicholas got up.

"I'm afraid I must be going," he said. "Thanks for the sherry and the sermon."

"I'd just like to add a word or two," said the vicar. "You may say—quite rightly—that the child is at present too young to understand any religious instruction, and will be for some years. True enough. But, unless you regularly see this child up till the age when he can begin to understand elementary teaching, what chance have you of teaching him anything? You must have his confidence before he'll learn anything from you. And he can't have confidence in you unless constantly in your company. So please grow up with this child until he is old enough to make decisions of his own. You will be well rewarded, I can promise you. The trust of an animal is a wonderful thing in life to have. The trust of a child is immeasurably greater. Please see that you all attain it. Then and then only will you be able to carry out the promises you made not an hour ago. So sorry you all have to go."

They said good-by and walked away in silence. Nothing could spoil Mary's happiness. Even the possibility that Sir Nicholas would never speak to any of them again. They could all feel the thunderclouds, and wondered when the storm would break. Sir Nicholas strode on in silence. But eventually he spoke.

"Hell and damnation," he said. "Hell and damnation," he repeated, "the fellow's right."

5 Call from a Stranger

HUGH WAS JUST OVER EIGHTEEN MONTHS OLD
when the adoption order was made. From that moment Mary's
happiness was as complete as human happiness can be. She
never ceased to be thankful for it. It never grew stale. She
never took it for granted. Her child and her husband. She had
them both. She wished that everyone could be as happy and,
kind and generous as she had been before Hugh became hers,
afterward she tried even harder to help the less fortunate.

It was a wonderful life. Bill loved to see Mary so happy and,
as Mrs. Lyndhurst had anticipated, began to take a far greater
interest in Hugh as he started to look and behave more like a
real person, and even to talk. Once Bill even missed a cricket
match to be with the boy.

One day, when Hugh was about two and a half, he was playing in the front garden when a stranger stopped to look at him.

"Hullo, young man," said the stranger, but Hugh regarded
him coldly, as children often do when someone out of their

world tries to draw them into conversation. The stranger was not offended.

"Having a good time?" he asked.

Hugh did not answer. Then Mary came out.

"Lovely boy you've got there," said the stranger.

"Thank you," said Mary. "We think so."

"Looks just like you," said the stranger. "The spitting image. Pity he's not a girl."

"D'you really think he's like me?" asked Mary.

"No doubt at all."

"Well, that's odd," said Mary. "He's adopted."

"You don't say," said the stranger. "No kidding?"

"It's a fact," said Mary.

"Well, it's an astonishing coincidence. I'd have sworn you were his mother. But I suppose a child grows to look a bit like the person who brings him up. Like husbands and wives grow to look like each other, in a way. They use the same expressions and look the same when they use them."

"I expect that's it," said Mary.

"He's a fine boy, anyway," said the stranger. "Aren't you frightened to leave him by himself in the front garden? Someone might run away with him."

"Nonsense," said Mary, "that doesn't happen in England."

"Not often, I agree. But it does happen. And little boys are quite valuable, you know. But he's a bit too old. For one thing, he can talk. No, on second thoughts, I think you're right."

"I'm glad to hear it," said Mary. "I think I'd go mad or something if I lost Hugh."

"Hugh, is it? A good name. They nearly called me Hugh, as a matter of fact. Well, I mustn't keep you. Good morning."

"Good morning," said Mary, and the stranger walked on.

A few days later he came again. He waited till Mary came out.

"Good morning," he said. "I was here the other morning."

"I remember," said Mary. "You were frightened at first that Hugh might be kidnapped."

"Yes. Silly of me. He's much too old. Adopted, I think you said. Forgive my asking, but how long did it take before you felt he was really yours? Or do you never feel for him as you would for your own child? I'm afraid I'm being very impertinent."

"Not at all," said Mary. "Hugh's been mine from the very first moment."

"Wonderful," said the stranger. "I wonder why his mother gave him up."

"Couldn't give him a proper home, I think," said Mary.

"What about the father?"

"Hasn't got one."

"Well, he must have one somewhere."

"I suppose so. But no one knows who he was. Just a casual acquaintance."

"I see. I'm afraid you must think it very odd of me to ask all these questions. As a matter of fact, I'm interested in adoption. Met a man once who . . . but I mustn't keep you. Good-by."

And he walked away.

The stranger repeated his visits until it became quite a normal thing for him to stop and chat with Mary over her front gate. After he'd been calling for a fortnight he said:

"D'you remember I once said I'd met a man?"

"Met a man?" asked Mary, not understanding.

"Just as I was going off one morning. I said I'd met a man who . . . and then I didn't finish the sentence."

"No," said Mary, "I don't remember."

The incident had made no impression on her.

"I told you I was interested in adoption."

"Yes, I remember you saying that."

"And then I started to tell you about a man but I didn't finish the sentence and went off."

"That's why I don't remember, I expect," said Mary. "But why are you telling me all this?"

"Only that the man is this boy's father. Forgive me, I must get on."

6 More About the Stranger

MARY WAS TERROR-STRICKEN. SHE RANG BILL AT
his office at once. He dropped everything and came home.

"What can it mean?" she asked desperately. "Is it a warning,
or a threat, or what?"

"There's nothing anyone can do," said Bill. "He's legally
ours and no one can take him away from us. That's certain."

"What about kidnapping?" said Mary. "He mentioned that
the first time I saw him. I thought he was just being silly. But
now it makes some horrible kind of sense."

"But, if anyone were going to kidnap the child, they wouldn't
come and say so first."

"That's true, of course. But then what does the man mean?
Or want?"

"Could be just a busybody. P'haps he likes hurting people,
or frightening them."

"But why did he come to us? How did he know Hugh was
adopted? Ah—I remember. He pretended that he thought Hugh

was just like me. I can see now. He did that to make me say
he was adopted. We've never pretended anything else, so I told
him."

"Well, there's only one thing to do," said Bill. "I'll speak
to the fellow myself. I'll soon find out what he's after."

"I'm so frightened."

"Now, that's one thing you needn't be. I tell you, nothing—
no one—can take Hugh away from us."

"I love to hear you say it—but what is he after?"

"I'll find that out. What time does he usually come?"

"It varies. Sometime between half-past ten and twelve."

"Right. The office'll have to take care of itself."

The next day Bill waited at home, but not in the garden.
They decided that he would not show himself until the man
had stopped to talk to Mary. Bill stayed at home all day but
the man never came. The same happened the next day.

"I can't stay at home forever," he said after that. "You give
me a ring when he comes. Try to keep him in conversation and
I'll nip back in a cab."

"It'll take you over half-an-hour. How'll I keep him that
long?"

"All right. I'll stay tomorrow."

But tomorrow produced no stranger. So Bill went back to the
office. Two days later the man appeared. Mary's heart jumped
when she saw him. He looked over the gate, saw her terrified
face, raised his hat, smiled, and walked on. She rushed to the
gate after him and then stopped. What could she say? If only
Bill were there. As if he had heard her, the man turned round
when he was twenty yards ahead, raised his hat again, smiled,
turned again, and went on.

Mary rushed into the house again and telephoned Bill. He
tried to comfort her, but comfort for her needed more than
words.

"I tell you what," he said, "we'll go straight round and see Mr. Luttrell. I'll ring from the office, to see if he's available, and I'll say it's urgent. But I'm sure there's nothing to be afraid of. Hugh is ours. Ours for always. Really."

This was a help to Mary. Something was going to be done. They were going to see a lawyer, and not merely *a* lawyer but the one who knew all about the case. After all, he had appeared for them before the judge. It's true that he had had to say nothing, but he was partly responsible for the order being made. He would see that Hugh remained theirs. Remained theirs? What a terrible thought even to imagine anything else. Suppose the man were the father himself? What could he do about it?

She waited for Bill's telephone call to confirm. She prayed that Mr. Luttrell would see them at once. While she waited, she comforted herself with remembering what Bill had said. Hugh is ours. Nothing can take him away. And then she terrified herself by imagining that they lost him. At last the telephone rang. It was all right. She could go straight round to Mr. Luttrell and Bill would meet her there. She didn't even change her clothes. It required an emergency of this kind to prevent her. All the same, as she hurried along to Mr. Luttrell's office, she felt sure that she was improperly dressed to appear before a solicitor. The fact that she did not even hesitate about the matter showed how desperate she was, as Mary was a woman who would almost have changed if there were a fire and she was not properly dressed for the neighbors to see.

She met Bill at the solicitor's office and he saw them at once.

"Now, what's all this?" he said, after shaking hands and getting them seated. "Have you changed your minds and want to hand the little fellow back? That can't be done, I'm afraid. But don't be upset. You can always put him out for adoption."

They hastily explained what had happened.

"I see," he said. "How very odd. I wonder what it's all about.

But don't distress yourselves. Nothing untoward can happen.
The adoption order was properly made. The mother consented.
She acknowledged receipt of the notice of the hearing and said
that she did not oppose the making of an order and did not
want to appear at the hearing. The father, whoever he is, had
no right to be heard and his consent wasn't necessary."

"Then what is this man doing? What does he want? Who
is he?"

"It's certainly strange," said Mr. Luttrell. "It can't be just
a coincidence that he's called on you. The chances against that
are millions, if not billions, to one."

"I don't quite understand."

"It's quite simple. Your case was conducted under a serial
number. That is to say, although your name and address and
everything about you was disclosed to the Court, the documents
served on the mother only contained a number. So she couldn't
tell who you were or where you lived. The father never had
any documents served on him at all. So he would know nothing
at all. All the mother would know is the Court that was asked
to make the order. Now, it is quite true that coincidences do
happen in life, but in my opinion it is absolutely impossible that
by pure coincidence the father or someone who knew him happened to look over your garden fence. The man who called on
you must have either known for certain that Hugh was your
adopted child or he must have had information very near to
that; for example, that you lived on that particular road or
something of the sort."

"But how could anyone find out?" asked Bill.

"That is certainly a question. But there, you do get odd coincidences. One person gets talking to another and the information that you have an adopted child which once belonged to a
woman called—called—well, of course, I don't remember the
name—called, well, whatever her name was—goes all over the

place, and it is certainly not beyond the bounds of possibility that the information reached by chance someone who knew the father. It isn't at all likely but it's not impossible, certainly not in a case where you've never concealed from anyone that Hugh is adopted. Such odd coincidences do occur and that one certainly can't be ruled out."

"But I thought you said it was billions to one," said Mary.

"Oh, no," said Mr. Luttrell. "What I say would be a billion-to-one chance is that the child's father, or someone who knew the child's father, casually wandering down your road should by chance stumble on the child and you. That is a virtual impossibility. We can rule it out."

"Then this man is the father, or someone who knows him?"

"Not necessarily, by any means. There are several possibilities. One is that he's a lunatic. That he makes a habit of chatting with strangers, finding out something about them and then frightening them if he can. For example, he may like frightening mothers of young children with the idea of kidnapping. Indeed, he tried that very thing on you. Then, when he found it was an adopted child, he thought it would be a good joke from his point of view to say he knew the father."

"But he couldn't tell that we didn't know who the father was," said Bill. "If he was just a stray lunatic, for all he knew we'd adopted a child of a widow. Or we'd adopted the child of a brother or sister or a hundred and one other things of that kind."

"Ah, but Mrs. Woodthorpe did tell him the father wasn't known," said Mr. Luttrell.

"Suppose he is the father or comes from him, what can he do?"

"Absolutely and precisely nothing," said Mr. Luttrell.

"Then what's he after?"

"Unless," went on Mr. Luttrell, and paused for a moment.

"Unless," he continued, "there was, for example, an affiliation order against the father or something of that sort."

"But there wasn't," said Mary.

The solicitor thought for a moment.

"Of course," he said, "we only have the mother's word for that. I suppose it's conceivable that she was telling lies. But, if that was the case, I'd have expected something to happen before now."

"Why?"

"Otherwise, the father would be paying money every week for nothing. Incidentally, that's quite a comforting thought. Suppose there was an affiliation order, but the mother lied about it in order to get rid of the child *and* keep the money. The father may have become suspicious and started to make inquiries. If he could prove adoption, his liability would be at an end."

"But surely," said Bill, "that would be a very odd way to go about it. Wouldn't he tell the Court, where he paid the money, what he suspected, and ask that the child should be produced? That would finish the mother. No need to go hunting round for the child."

"True enough," said Mr. Luttrell. "By the same token, the mother might want to borrow the child to show at the Magistrate's Court. But that's really very farfetched. We can debate about this for hours, but we shan't get any further until the man has told us a bit more. You'll have to stop him and ask him."

"Suppose he never comes again?"

"Then you've nothing to worry about. But, unless he's just a lunatic, he or someone else will come again. And you must tackle him about it. Better still, your husband should."

"But I can't stay at home every day," said Bill.

"I quite see that, but perhaps you could manage a fortnight, say. If he doesn't come within that time, I doubt if he'll call again. If he does come, find out what he wants and what he knows, and come and tell me."

"You don't think we should go to the police?"

"Certainly not at the moment. As far as one can tell, the man hasn't broken the law in any way. He has simply said that he knows the father of your child. True or false, it isn't a crime to say that."

"Mr. Luttrell," said Mary, "if there was an affiliation order, what could the father do?"

"Nothing very effective, I'm sure," said Mr. Luttrell.

"But you said he couldn't do anything unless there was an affiliation order. That means he could do something if there was."

"Well, strictly speaking," said Mr. Luttrell, "a man who is liable to contribute to the maintenance of a child by virtue of an order or agreement is entitled to be heard on the question whether or not an adoption order should be made. If there was an affiliation order, the father was entitled to be served with your application for adoption and to appear before the judge and say why he objected, if he did object. Strictly speaking, then, if he wasn't served with your application he could, I suppose, apply to have the order set aside."

"The affiliation order?"

"No, I mean the adoption order. Hold on a minute, Mrs. Woodthorpe—it's not . . ."

Mary had nearly fainted. When she recovered, she said:

"But I thought you said there was nothing effective he could do. And now you say he could set aside the adoption order. That means we'd lose Hugh. I can't lose him. I won't."

"Please don't get too distressed, Mrs. Woodthorpe. Although technically he might have the right to apply to set the adoption order aside, unless he could show some good reason why it should not be made again, the Court in order to avoid circuity of action would refuse to set aside the order."

"I just don't understand," said Mary. "And now you're starting to use long words. Circu-something, what on earth does that mean? And why wasn't all this thought of long ago? Why wasn't the father found and asked about it before we had the order?"

"Now, please don't get upset," said Mr. Luttrell. "I'm sure you'll have nothing to worry about."

"Nothing to worry about!" said Mary. "My whole life, our whole lives are concerned, and you say there's nothing to worry about. I'm beginning to think that this easy judge what's-his-name, who didn't worry about technicalities, wasn't such a good idea after all."

"I've never had a case like this before," said Mr. Luttrell.

"Well, you've got one now," said Mary. "At least, I'm not sure that you have. Perhaps we should go . . ."

"Now, darling," said Bill, "Mr. Luttrell is doing his best for us, and has done it all along. Let's do what he says and see what this fellow's really after."

"I'm sorry," said Mary. "I didn't mean to be rude. But I just can't tell you how I feel."

"I quite understand," said Mr. Luttrell. "Give me a ring as soon as you have any more news."

They left the office and went home, Bill comforting Mary as best he could.

"I'm sure we're making too heavy weather of this," he said. "It's so easy to imagine things. Anyway, I'll stay at home for a fortnight."

A few days later Mary, who had watched for the man every day and almost all day, saw the man coming down the street. She told Bill, who had waited inside the house. The man came

along, took off his hat to Mary, smiled, and went on. Mary
went inside the house at once.

"Quick, after him," she said.

Bill went out and soon caught up with him.

"Excuse me," he said. "Might I have a word with you?"

The man stopped and turned to look at Bill.

"Yes?" he said inquiringly.

"You've been talking to my wife," Bill said.

"The charming young woman just down the road with the
just as charming child? Yes, certainly. But I assure you I don't
know her and there was nothing improper about it."

"You told her you know the father of the child."

"Yes," said the man.

"How do you know him?"

"Before I answer that, would you tell me any reason why I
should?"

"You've frightened the life out of my wife, and I'm entitled
to know."

"Frightened the life out of her? Quite unintentional, I assure
you. I'm so sorry. Please assure her that I didn't mean to."

"Who are you, and what d'you want?"

"Why on earth should I say who I am and what I want? My
car hasn't run into yours, or anything like that. Why should I
give you my name and address? I don't mind telling you my
wants, though. The same as nearly everyone else's. Now, if
you'll excuse me, I'd like to continue my stroll."

"I must know what you want and what you know."

"Must you?" said the man, and started to walk on.

Bill followed him.

"Would you mind?" said the man, "or must I call a policeman? You're beginning to annoy me."

"I'm sorry," said Bill, "I don't want to annoy you. I just

want to understand. My wife is desperately worried. Surely you'd want to help her?"

The man stopped.

"Well," he said, "that's rather a different attitude to adopt. To help a lady in distress is one thing. To be bullied is another." He paused for a moment and then repeated quickly: "I won't be bullied."

"Perhaps you'd be very kind and come back with me then," said Bill. "Come and have a chat and a drink."

"Now, that's very civil of you. I should enjoy it. And to see your wife again. I do congratulate you on her. You're very lucky."

Bill rather preferred the man's aggressive to his oily attitude, but he could see that he would get nothing out of him unless he played the game the man's way. So he gave in with as good a grace as possible.

They walked back to the house. Mary was waiting for them.

"I'm afraid I can't introduce you," began Bill, "but . . ."

"Baines," said the man, "Archie Baines. Baines is all right, but I hate Archie. It's not even Archibald. Believe it or not, I was christened Archie."

"May I introduce Mr. Baines?" said Bill. "My wife."

"We're old friends," said the man. "How nice to see you again. I've enjoyed our chats."

"I've asked Mr. Baines to have a glass of sherry with us."

She could not say: "How nice." So she said nothing and led them into the sitting room, where she produced sherry and glasses.

"Your health," said the man, "and the young man's."

They each sipped their sherry.

"And now," said the man, "I believe I can be of some service to you. Pray tell me how."

No one spoke for several seconds. Then Mary said:

"You said the other day that you know Hugh's father. Is that a fact?"

"It would be a very strange thing to say if it weren't." He paused. "Yes, it's a fact," he added.

"Who is he?"

"I'm not sure that I ought to tell you. It might be betraying a professional confidence."

"Are you his—his lawyer then?"

"Oh dear, no. But thank you for the compliment, if indeed it is a compliment to look like a lawyer."

"His accountant?"

"No such luck. If you can call mine a profession, it's pretty low in the hierarchy of professions. We have no institute or institution, not even an association. I'm an inquiry agent, as a matter of fact. Even bookmakers have an association. Several, in fact. Perhaps we will one day. How does R.I.P.I. sound? The Royal Institution of Private Investigators. I like the R.I.P., anyway. We're such peaceable fellows."

"You're an inquiry agent then?" asked Bill.

"Not entirely—but in this matter, yes."

"Is Hugh anything to do with your inquiries?"

"Yes and no."

"Could you explain what you mean?"

"I'm afraid not. Not at the moment, anyway. What excellent sherry."

An awkward silence followed. Mary hardly dared to ask the questions she wanted to ask, lest the answers should make things worse. But worst of all was not to know.

Eventually she started:

"Does he—does he—the father, I mean, know about Hugh?"

"Well—a father ought to, shouldn't he?"

"D'you mean he knows that Hugh is ours?"

"I didn't say that. You asked if the father knew about Hugh.

Well, if you have a baby, a father should know it—not as well as the mother, of course, but well enough."

"He might not. I mean, if he just met a girl at a dance."

"I see what you mean. Just a casual one-day affair. Is that what you mean?"

"Yes."

"You think that's the father in this case?"

"We were told so."

"I see."

"Isn't it correct?"

"Let me think," said the man. "Ought I to tell you or would it be a breach of our code? In spite of the absence of any R.I.P.I., we have a strict code, you know. I know a lot of people don't like us and judges sometimes say the most horrible things about us. We have, of course, some black sheep among us, but we're certainly not as bad as people think. For example, we rarely invent evidence. Certainly not if we can get it the proper way. No short cuts, I mean. Of course, if we come up against an absolutely blank wall—well, human nature being what it is, we might stretch a point. But what were you asking me? I'm digressing. You don't want an exposition of the morals of an inquiry agent, do you?"

"We asked if Hugh was the result of a casual affair," said Bill.

"I really don't see why I shouldn't tell you that. No, for the life of me I don't. But I must be sure about it. Can't recall the spoken word, you know. Once I've said it, I've said it. Once you know it, you know it. No use telling my client I'm sorry, I didn't mean to and all that, if he's told me not to tell you. Now, has he? It should be in my files, if he has. But I haven't got them here. Perhaps, after all, I'd better let the matter stand over. I'll be passing here again, no doubt, and you could ask me then. I must make a point of looking up my files. How to remember?"

He took out a handkerchief and tied a knot in it.

"An old method," he said, "but I find it pretty effective. Unless, of course, I lose the thing, or throw it in the laundry basket as soon as I get home. Now, I really mustn't keep you any more. It's been so kind of you."

"But why are you interested in the child?" asked Bill.

"It's a nice child."

"There are plenty of those."

"That's a great comfort, isn't it?" said the man. "Plenty more where that came from."

Mary went white. She clenched a chair with her hands and almost whispered:

"Are you trying to take Hugh away from us?"

"Me personally? Good gracious, no. What should I want with a baby? No offense, and all that, but *I* don't want him."

"Does the father?"

"I suppose he might, if he knew."

"Then he doesn't know."

"Good gracious, no. Not yet. I'm very particular about giving information. Got to be certain first, haven't I? Suppose I told a man it was his child and it wasn't, I'd be in for it, wouldn't I? I'll tell you something. Don't you envy my self-control? Here am I being cross-examined up hill and down dale by you two—in the nicest possible way, of course. But it's I, really, who ought to be asking you questions. And I haven't asked a thing. That's pretty good, isn't it? Now, I really must be going. No, please don't show me out. No doubt I'll be seeing you again soon."

He got up, took his hat and went quickly out of the door, out of the gate and up the street.

7 The Stranger Calls Again

AS SOON AS HE HAD GONE, MARY CLUNG TO BILL
for help. For a short time she sobbed uncontrollably. He held
her in silence. After she had recovered, he said:

"We must go to Luttrell at once."

"What can he do?"

"At least advise us on the next step."

They were not able to arrange an interview with the solicitor
until the next morning, but he saw them then and they told
him what had happened.

"One thing is certain, I'm afraid," he said. "He will come
again."

"What is his object?"

"Well, I can't know for certain and I don't want to alarm
you but, I think, blackmail."

"Blackmail?"

"Mind you, as I say, there's nothing certain about it, but
what I *think* is this: This man, whether he's the father himself

or, as he says, an inquiry agent, or neither, has found out that you adopted Hugh. It's possible he knows no more than that."

"But surely . . ."

"Nearly every adoptive parent can be scared at the thought of losing the child. However much he or she may have been advised that the adoption order is binding, once the possibility of there having been some legal hitch gets into their mind, many of them would become terrified at the thought of losing the child. A happily married couple who have their own child cannot be deprived of it by law, unless they ill-treat it. So you can't blackmail ordinary parents, except by kidnapping. And that's a very difficult and dangerous operation. But an adopted child is another matter. Not even a lawyer knows all the law or anything like it. How can a layman tell what it is? I'll guarantee that, if you took the simplest case, for example, where both the father and mother of the child had consented in writing to the adoption, the adoptive parents would, at least, be shaken by being told by a stranger that the adoption order wasn't binding and could be set aside. Of course, in such a case they'd go to their lawyers and find that it was just a try-on, as it may well be here. But they'd be shaken at first. First-class material for blackmail. This man may make a habit of it."

"But surely he'd have been caught long ago," said Bill. "When the people he's started on find out that they've nothing to fear, they'd go to the police and he'd be trapped."

"That's true," said Mr. Luttrell, "but you may be his first victims."

"Mr. Luttrell," said Mary, "if this man is going to try to blackmail us, and if we have him prosecuted, can you assure me absolutely that there is no chance, no chance whatever, of our losing Hugh?"

"If he's the father, none whatever."

"Then if he's not the father?"

Mr. Luttrell thought for a short time. His very silence conveyed his answer to Mary. Before he could speak, she said:

"Then there is a chance, if he's not the father?"

"Mrs. Woodthorpe, I hate to see anyone as anxious as you are, but I should not be doing my duty if I simply said that there was no chance whatever. I think it highly improbable, but I cannot in all honesty say that there is no chance whatever. I'm afraid that I'm beginning to agree with what you said at an earlier interview. It may well have been a pity this case didn't come before Judge Hazlewell."

"Exactly what difference would it have made?" asked Bill.

"Well, he would have insisted on careful inquiries being made about the father. He wouldn't have accepted the mere word of the mother. The inquiries might have led nowhere and the mother might have stuck to her story. If that had happened, we'd be no better off than we are now, though you would have had the consolation—such as it would have been—that everything had been done to prevent this situation arising. But I have to admit that, in the majority of cases, where Judge Hazlewell isn't satisfied with the mother's story, the truth is arrived at before the order is made, and the father is found."

"And what difference would that have made?"

"It would have meant that either the father consented to the adoption, in which case he couldn't make trouble afterward, or that he objected to it. If he had objected, his objections would have been gone into fully then. If the judge had rejected them, then, unless he appealed, the order would have been as foolproof as if he had not objected. If he had appealed and had his appeal dismissed, it would have been the same as if he had not appealed. If, however, the judge or the Court of Appeal had allowed his objection, and refused to make an adoption order, undoubtedly you would have suffered great distress. But the child would only have been with you then for a few months. I know that even then it would have been a terrible blow to you, but nothing compared with what it would be now."

"Why d'you tell us all this now?" asked Bill. "Why not when we first came to you?"

"A very fair question," said Mr. Luttrell. "And this is the answer. It is perfectly true that, before Judge Hazlewell makes an adoption order, he tries to tie up all the loose ends and to ensure that a situation like this can never arise."

"Then surely it would have been better . . ."

"Please let me finish," said Mr. Luttrell. "The reason that I advised you to have the case heard before the other judge is this. In the first place, I knew that you, like every other adopting mother, wanted the order made as quickly as possible. I knew, too, that any adjournment of the case would inevitably have made you anxious and unhappy. That's true, isn't it?"

"Yes," said Bill, "that is quite true."

"Well now, I have to tell you that, although, as I said, Judge Hazlewell's methods do often result in a putative father being found, I have never yet known a case where, when found, he objected. Sometimes he denied the paternity, which was just as good as a consent. Sometimes he was very angry at being found, but on no single occasion, and my experience is considerable, has he attempted to prevent the making of an adoption order. I need hardly tell you also that I have never come across a case like yours before. Naturally, in future . . ."

But Mary broke in:

"In future! What does that matter to us?"

"You're quite right, Mrs. Woodthorpe. My actions in the future are no consolation to you. But you're entitled to an explanation from me and I'm entitled to give it. I had to weigh-up your unhappiness and anxiety, if the case had been adjourned, against the possibility that this might happen, something which to my knowledge had never happened before. It was in the highest degree unlikely that the father, if found, would object. We still have no reason to think that he will object. It was also in the highest degree unlikely that any blackmailer would ever be able to find out who you were or where the child was. I can only say that, although with this present experience of yours before me I should warn the client of this most unlikely possibility, I should be perfectly prepared to do the same again unless the client, after being warned by me, preferred to take no chances."

"Shouldn't you have told us of the risk, however small, of going before Judge Bramcote?" asked Bill.

"It's easy to be wise after the event. Certainly I shall tell my clients in the future. But I must admit that I never contemplated such a possibility. It's a chance in a hundred thousand. I considered Judge Hazlewell to be too persnickity. I freely admit that he has himself given as a reason for the attitude he adopts the possibility that something like this might happen. But I'm afraid that, as a result of my experience that it never *did* happen, I discounted the possibility."

"So what do we do now?" asked Bill.

"Well, if it's blackmail, we must go to the police," said Mr. Luttrell, "but there isn't really any evidence of this at the moment. What you'll have to do is to let him talk and, as soon as any suggestion of money comes into it, come back to me, or go straight to the police yourselves."

"And what will they do?" asked Mary.

"They'll set a trap for the man, with your cooperation. And, if he's caught, he'll go to prison for a long time, as he'll richly deserve."

"Won't he have to be tried first?"

"Of course."

"And we'll have to give evidence?"

"I'm afraid so."

"Thank you for being so frank, Mr. Luttrell," said Bill, but Mary said nothing.

After a little further conversation Bill and Mary went home.

"I'm sure it'll be all right," said Bill, "and I'm longing to see that chap in jail."

"I don't mind whether he goes to prison or not, so long as we're safe with Hugh."

"We're certain to be," said Bill. "I know what a strain it is on you, darling, but, believe me, it'll be all right. Would you like me to stay at home for a fortnight again?"

"No," said Mary, "I don't think so. Now that I've met him with you, I think I can manage."

"Ring me as soon as he's left then," said Bill.

"You bet," said Mary.

A week went by and Mary did not ring Bill. A fortnight and still she didn't.

"I think he's given up," said Bill. "Give me a kiss and look happy."

She kissed him and tried to look happy, but it was not a great success.

A month went by. Mary looked worse and worse. Three months and she was no better.

"Look, darling," said Bill, "we'll go for a holiday. You can't forget about that horrible man, but he's left us now for good. Hugh's our own forever. Why so miserable? You've both of us."

Mary burst into tears.

"Darling, what is it?"

"Nothing, really. I'm so happy, I expect."

But she certainly did not look it.

Bill returned to the holiday theme.

"Let's go somewhere really far away. I'll take three weeks off. Now. Anywhere you like. You go and make the reservations. Anywhere at all. Don't bother what it costs."

"It sounds wonderful," said Mary. "I shall love it. Just to get away. With you and Hugh. It's sweet of you. Three whole weeks."

She seemed to look happier than she had for a long time. Just before he left, she said:

"Will you give me a check for the deposits?"

"You pay it, darling, and I'll give it back to you."

"All right," she said, and then added:

"As a matter of fact, I'm a bit low in my account at the moment. I would prefer to have a check."

"Of course, but I haven't one with me. I'll bring one home tonight and you can go tomorrow."

On the way to the office, happy that Mary had for once looked more herself, Bill suddenly thought about her saying that her account was a bit low. That's very odd, he said to himself. He made Mary a substantial quarterly allowance and, in addition, she had quite a reasonable income of her own. She spent quite a lot on clothes, but she had never appeared short of money before. A horrible thought crossed his mind. He went to the office, collected his checkbook and went straight home.

He found Mary in tears.

"Is this what you do all day?" he asked.

She nodded miserably.

"I've brought my checkbook," he said, "and not, I think, before it's time."

She looked at him sharply. He had never seen her look quite like that.

"You've been buying him off, haven't you?" he said.

She sobbed. The relief that he knew was coupled with fear of what he might do. He took her on his lap, like a child, and let her sob on his shoulder. When she was quiet, he said softly:

"Now tell me all about it, darling."

"You won't do anything?" she asked fearfully. "Promise."

"Darling, I won't do anything that won't help. That I promise."

"But you'll think it'll help and you'll be wrong . . . and— and—"

She burst into tears again. Then she steadied herself:

"I want to tell you, oh so much. It's been terrible. But you must promise first."

"All right," he said, "I promise."

"He's been coming here ever since that day."

"Did he ask for anything?"

"Not really. I offered."

"What did you say?"

"I said it would be worth a lot to me if the father never knew. Then he said he had his duty to do. So I said: 'Can't I employ you?' 'As what?' he said. 'As an anti-inquiry agent,' I said. 'That's a novel proposition,' he said. 'What are your usual charges?' I asked. 'I haven't any usual charges,' he said. 'It all depends on the case and the client.' 'Well, the case is that I don't want the father to know, and the client is me.' "

"How much have you paid him altogether?"

"Over seven hundred pounds."

"It's just as well I came home."

"But you've promised not to do anything."

"Then what's the good of my coming home?"

"What's the good? Why, you can help me pay now. Now that you know, everything's going to be all right."

For once Mary looked almost cheerful.

"You mean," said Bill, "that we're to go on paying this fellow for the rest of our lives?"

"Gracious, no," said Mary, "only till Hugh is sixteen. I'd got it worked out that with my capital I could manage for seven years. But then his charges started to go up. But, now you're in it too, it'll be fine."

"D'you realize what sort of a man we're dealing with? By the time Hugh is sixteen we'll probably have paid him at least twenty-five thousand pounds."

Mary smiled cheerfully.

"But you've got more than that, darling. And you can cut down my allowance. Oh, this is wonderful. I am lucky to have such a husband. I'm sure a lot wouldn't stand for it."

Bill looked blankly in front of him. Mary really meant it. He had a good income and about forty thousand pounds capital. What was twenty-five thousand pounds compared with Mary's happiness? It was an awful lot of money to pay to a scoundrel but, if it would make Mary happy, he'd do it. And what was the alternative? A prosecution. The father would then be almost certain to learn, and what would happen then? No one can tell. Mr. Luttrell's talk about circuity of action had been almost as baffling to him as it was to Mary. But, on the other hand, the father mightn't be interested at all. This might be just a blackmailer who'd accidentally got on to a good thing, and was pretending he knew the father and that the father wanted inquiries made. To pay twenty-five thousand pounds to prevent an application to set aside the adoption order was one thing. He would do it cheerfully. But to be swindled out of it for nothing was another matter. Bill had an idea. It was not breaking his promise to Mary to keep it to himself.

"I'm so glad you've told me," said Bill. "Of course, Hugh is worth twenty-five thousand pounds and more—all I've got, in fact."

"Darling," she said, and for the first time in months smiled really happily.

"Now, I'm not going to let you bear the burden any longer. I'm going to pay the chap myself. I may even be able to do a deal with him. A lump sum not to come again."

"Wonderful," said Mary.

"When will he be here again?" he asked.

"Next Friday, I expect," she said.

"Right," said Bill, "I'll be here."

"You have promised not to tell, haven't you? Not Mr. Luttrell, or the police, or anyone?"

"Of course," he said.

He waited patiently for next Friday.

8 A Nice Round Sum

THE MAN WHO CALLED HIMSELF BAINES ARRIVED
almost exactly when he was expected. He had begun to look
forward to these interviews. He found the exercise of power
exciting and the result of such exercise most remunerative. But
greed is the ruin of the criminal. He comes too often or asks
too much. In blackmail it seems so easy. Why on earth should
one labor with one's body or mind seven or eight hours a day
to gain a comparatively small sum when, by the sweet use of
power, one can get more in a quarter of an hour?

It was upon this known greed of blackmailers that Bill was
banking. He realized, of course, that he would have to be most
discreet when he first came upon the scene, or the man might
expect a trap, take fright and disappear. Though his disappear-
ance would be a considerable gain, there would always remain
with Mary a lingering fear until the exact amount of the man's
knowledge, and any purpose for which he had come other than
blackmail, was known. So he must play him gently until the
right moment.

Mary let the man in and took him to the sitting room. He did not give any sign that he was affected by seeing Bill. He was too controlled for that, but he must have been shocked.

"Good morning," said Bill.

"Nice to see you again," said the man.

"I'd rather like to have a talk with you alone for a few minutes," said Bill. "Darling, will you go and play with Hugh in the front?"

Mary and Hugh went outside where they were in full view of the men inside the room. Bill closed the window. The windows were double-glazed and this ensured that they could not be heard. It was important to do this openly, so that the man's suspicions of a trap might be allayed. After all, a husband and wife are two witnesses, a husband only one. Unless there were someone concealed somewhere, or unless there were microphones in the room, the suggested interview must look reasonably innocent.

"Well now," said Bill, "I understand my wife has been employing you. A sort of counterespionage."

"You can put it that way, but I haven't asked her for a penny."

"Who said you had? I'm quite satisfied that whatever she's paid you was paid by her entirely voluntarily. Indeed, it was her suggestion."

"I'm glad you recognize that."

"Of course."

"Then what is it you want?"

"Just a business talk. I wanted to see if we could do a deal for a lump sum. For one thing, I don't think it does Mary any good having these regular meetings. For another, it's getting expensive. Now, I'm not rich but I'm not poor, and I'd be prepared to settle once and for all for a largish cash payment. Let me make it plain that I'm offering this. You're not asking it."

"Would you put that in writing?"

"Willingly, if we can agree on a figure. Now, I look at it this way," said Bill. "I'm not an actuary but it's possible to look at things actuarially from a layman's point of view. Say we want to cover the next twelve years. At the present rate of striking I'd say that Mary would be paying you between one thousand and two thousand pounds a year. What would you say to twenty thousand?"

Once again the man was able to prevent his true reactions to the suggestion being noticed.

"You were saying?" he said.

"Twenty-five thousand," said Bill.

"I didn't quite catch," said the man.

"I don't think I could go above thirty thousand."

"Did you say thirty, or forty?"

"Forty."

"I think that might be arranged," said the man.

He would have been very content with a suggestion of five thousand pounds. After all, he could always come again when that was exhausted. He'd willingly have stayed away for a month or two, or even more, for five thousand. But, when Bill mentioned twenty thousand, he could see a completely different life opening for him. And, if a man will start the bidding at twenty thousand, he'll go a long way beyond. With forty thousand pounds he could even afford to start life abroad and really drop the Woodthorpes. It was a chance too good to be missed. He decided he would put it up to fifty thousand. If a man will pay forty, he'll pay fifty. And fifty was a nice round sum. Bill allowed himself to be raised to fifty thousand pounds.

"I'll have to sell some securities," he said, "but I can let you have it in a week, I should think. And I dare say you'd like that little bit I said I'd put in writing."

"Thank you. There's no need to mention the amount."

"Of course not," said Bill. "How will this do? 'Any sums handed by me or my wife to Mr. Baines' . . . I forget your Christian name."

"Never mind. Baines will do."

" '. . . handed by me to Mr. Baines were entirely our own idea and handed over absolutely voluntarily.' How's that?"

"Yes, I think that will do."

Bill wrote it out on a piece of paper and handed it over.

"Now, perhaps we'll have my wife in and tell her we've settled everything."

He called Mary and she came at once.

"Mr. Baines and I have settled the matter once and for all, darling," he said.

"Oh—good," said Mary.

"I'm going to give him a lump sum in about a week. I'll give it to you and you can hand it to him."

"I'm so glad," said Mary. "Then it's all settled."

"Indeed, yes," said the man. "I must admit that I've enjoyed our chats. But all good things come to an end. But there'll be one more. In a week, I think you said? I'll be here. Same time. Good day," and he left.

"You are clever," said Mary. "How much are you going to give him?"

Bill hesitated.

"I'm afraid it's rather a lot. He fairly put the screws on me and there was nothing I could do but agree."

"But how much? Over a thousand?"

"Hold tight, darling. And let me say first I don't grudge a penny of it, if it makes you happy."

"How much?" said Mary.

"Er—fifty thousand pounds," said Bill.

"You're joking."

"I'm afraid not."

"But it's impossible. It'll be pretty well all you have."

"Hugh and you are worth much more, and I've got you both."

"But I can't let you do it. Fifty thousand pounds! It's impossible. What an utter blackguard! Oh, I could bite him, I hate him so!"

"I doubt if he'd taste very nice."

"But what can we do? I'm not going to let you be ruined. How can we prevent it?"

"Well, of course, we could—but you hate the idea so."

"Could what? Go to the police, you mean?"

"Well, we *could,* but I wouldn't dream of it unless you wanted to."

"Oh, darling, it's so awful," said Mary. "But you're quite right. We must go to them. I can't think why I was so silly before. They'll let us keep Hugh, won't they?"

"Of course, they will. I don't suppose he even knows the father. And, even if he does, the father doesn't want Hugh or he'd have done something before."

Mary brightened at that.

"Yes, I suppose he would. He could have gone to the Court, couldn't he?"

"He'd have to find out which it was, but he could do that quite easily from the mother. I'm sure there's nothing to worry about except this ruffian, and we'll soon put him where he belongs. Let's go round to the police now."

Bill thought it as well to get things started, in case Mary should change her mind. However, she showed no signs of doing so and, within a few days, a reception committee had been arranged for Archie Baines.

9 The Final Call

MEANWHILE, THE MAN IN QUESTION WAS GETTING more and more elated. He was a petty criminal, one of whose parents appeared in *Who's Who*. He had been sent to a public school but allowed to leave early, because he was ambitious to "get on." As his father had had practically no education but had at a comparatively early age made vast sums of money in business of one kind or another, he had no objection to his son's trying to do the same. But neither he nor his wife gave any time to their boy's upbringing. They had none to give, the father being occupied in making more and more money (with no obvious object except possibly a barony), the mother being equally occupied in organizing social functions for various charities. All they had done for Eric was to give him money, and, when he had disgraced them sufficiently often, they paid him off on condition that he change his name to Smith. The parting was on a purely business basis.

"As my son," said Eric's father, "I won't give you another

penny. As Eric Smith—deed poll and all that, and I'll want to see it first—as Eric Smith you can have five thousand pounds, and get out."

Eric produced the deed poll and his father produced the five thousand pounds. It seemed a lot at the time but it was not long before he needed more. So he traded on an educated accent—the only thing he had acquired at school—and his reasonably good looks, and started to make money how he could.

When it was stated in the newspapers that Eric Smith had been sent to prison, it meant nothing to his parents. It mightn't even be their son. There must be a good many Eric Smiths in prison. But he did not often find his way into the national press, his crimes being of no general interest.

And now he was really going to crown his career. Fifty thousand pounds, and in one venture. He could start life all over again. He'd go into a legitimate business somewhere. Perhaps even marry and settle down. He conjured up wonderful visions of the future. Cars, women, hotels, sandy beaches, luxury air travel—the lot. He hadn't done so badly, after all. What a bit of luck that he'd been told about the Woodthorpes. He never dreamed it would be so easy. If ever there was a piece of cake, this was it. He even thought of sending his father five thousand pounds with a rude message. On second thoughts, he decided to send the rude message only. From the most expensive hotel in the Bahamas. But just a letter wouldn't do, or his father would think he'd simply got a job in the hotel or something. Anyway, that could take care of itself. In a week's time he'd have fifty thousand pounds. Almost as much as his father had made at the same age.

He could hardly wait for the week to go by. He even thought of paying a midweek call just to encourage the lady. There's no doubt she was terrified of him. It gave him a pleasant tingling sensation when he remembered his visits and thought of her white, frightened face. He could have made her do anything. And all for a stupid little toddler who might easily be killed in a road accident within a year or two. Or have pneumonia and die. It was not surprising that Eric, thinking of his own home, was contemptuous of mother love.

Mary's husband hadn't appeared frightened, but obviously he wanted to protect his wife. Perhaps Eric should have asked for seventy-five thousand pounds, or even a hundred thousand. He'd got the chap up to fifty thousand pretty quickly. And without asking for a penny. Yes, he thought, it's a pity I didn't run him up a bit more. Perhaps I can still. But perhaps it's better not to. Every man must have his limit, and, if you go beyond it, he may go for the police. But she'd never let him, he told himself. He had quite cleverly, without actually referring to the police, made it quite plain to Mary that, if she went for help, she'd stand a good chance of losing Hugh.

He thought back on it. He'd really been very clever. Not a threat, not a demand. Should he put them up to one hundred thousand? Take the fifty thousand and say that next week there must be another? It was deliciously tempting. The father had gone up so easily to fifty, he must be a very rich man. What's another fifty to a millionaire? But then he told himself that the Woodthorpes' road and house, though pleasant, did not look as though they were connected with a millionaire. No, he mustn't be greedy. And, after all, he'd got them up from twenty to fifty thousand. Not bad for a tyro. Blackmail was quite new to him. How some of the petty criminals he'd met would have envied him. They might have but, oddly enough, the hardened big-time criminal would have despised him. Blackmail is not a popular crime with the professional criminal. Not with one of class, anyway.

Gradually the week went by and at last the great day came. He dressed particularly well that day. He'd do it in style. Itching to have his hands on the fifty thousand, he nevertheless managed to stroll down the road as though he were in no hurry at all. He got a pleasant sensation out of controlling himself, different from the sensation of power over Mary but in a way akin to it. He slowed down even more. It was like a small boy counting to fifty before he eats a beautiful dessert.

At last he reached the house and Mary was waiting for him.

"My husband's at the office," she said. "He hoped you wouldn't mind."

Mind, he thought; that's a good one.

"Not at all," he said. "I've enjoyed our little conversations solo."

"Then do sit down and have a glass of sherry."

This was not at all what he wanted. Squeezing Mary in the past for small sums was fun. But he wanted this fifty thousand in his hands as quickly as possible. So that he could go home and count it, yes, and gloat over it. But it wouldn't do to appear too impatient.

"That's very kind," he said and sat down.

"There's just one thing," said Mary as she gave him the sherry. "There really will be no chance of the father learning where Hugh is if we hire you as suggested?"

"You can forget all about the father. There is no father. Never was any father."

Mary was startled.

"You mean you only made it up?"

"Good gracious, no," said Eric. "All I mean is that, with me on your side, the only father this boy will ever know is at his office, and his name . . . I'll give you one guess . . . no, I won't. It's Woodthorpe."

"Thank you," said Mary. "Then you'll certainly earn our most grateful thanks."

A bit more than thanks, thought Eric, but it didn't do to say so.

"Don't mention it. It's just a business transaction."

After a moment he added, when he found the delay becoming insupportable:

"Talking of which, I wonder . . ."

He was very careful to use no words of demand. Just suppose they had gone to the police, he wasn't making any evidence against himself. He'd always treated each interview as though it were being overheard. No demands, no threats. He made all the pressure come from Mary. But now she was being difficult. Perhaps *she* was trying to get her money's worth. Trying to get him to beg like a dog. He'd once heard of a wife who made her husband do that when he wanted anything. But he mustn't fall for that. Just in case.

"Yes," said Mary, "you were wondering?"

"Just about our little bit of business."

"Of course," said Mary. "Fifty thousand pounds, it was."

"Was it?" he said in a tired voice, as though the whole thing were rather a bore. "Was it then? Well, if you say so, I'm quite happy about it."

But although Mary mentioned the money, she made no attempt to get it. He looked round the room. There was a fat envelope on the desk. But not fat enough. If it was all in fivers, then there'd be ten thousand of them. Quite a package. He had asked for some pound notes, but he hadn't pressed it too hard in case it made them think he was frightened. But fivers would be all right, if you were careful. All the same, he'd brought a suitcase in case it was only partly in fivers.

"Before you go," said Mary, "I wonder if you'd tell me something about the father?"

A sudden thought occurred to him.

"I might get you some information about him, but I'd have to pay for it."

"I see," said Mary. "I'm afraid we can't run to any more."

Oh well, he thought, perhaps I was right not to be greedy. But when is she going to cough it up? I'm tired of this.

"Nice little place you have here," he forced himself to say.

"You still like it?" she said. "I'm glad. We do. But is there nothing you already know about the father which you can tell me? After all, it won't cost you anything to tell me what you know. And how did you find out that we had his child?"

"That would be telling," said Eric.

"Of course," said Mary, "and I do wish you'd tell me."

"Sorry, Mrs. Woodthorpe," said Eric. "I keep faith with all my clients. I'll keep faith with you by concealing your address and identity, and I'll keep faith with my other client by doing exactly the same for him. What could be fairer?"

"Very well," said Mary. "Now, I mustn't keep you any more. Good-by."

She got up and held out her hand.

"But," said Eric, "but . . ."

"Yes?" said Mary.

"There was a parcel, wasn't there?"

"Of course, how stupid of me. It's in the hall. In brown paper. Perhaps you'd pick it up as you go out. Good-by again."

She showed him out of the room, and there was the brown paper parcel. Just about the right size, he reckoned. Good. At last. I'd have burst if we'd gone on talking any longer. He picked it up, put it in his suitcase and walked out of the house. Now for home, he said to himself. And there's going to be no strolling back either. I want to get my hands on the stuff. There was no taxi in sight. So he would have to walk till he found one.

He had gone about two hundred yards when a police car stopped beside him and two officers got out.

"Excuse me, sir," said one of them. "Would you mind telling me what's in that suitcase?"

God! thought Eric. But, thank heaven, I've made no demands. No threats. They can't get me for this. I've lost the fifty thousand pounds. No Bahamas this time. But they're not going to get me.

"Certainly, officer," he said as calmly and slowly as he could, though it was not too easy. "I've got a parcel with fifty thousand pounds in notes in it. I'd rather not open it here for obvious reasons. Might blow away."

"Perhaps you wouldn't mind coming to Scotland Yard, sir, and opening it there," said the officer.

"Scotland Yard?" said Eric. "What on earth for?"

"A complaint has been made that you demanded fifty thousand pounds from Mr. and Mrs. Woodthorpe with menaces."

"Quite untrue," said Eric. "They offered it me quite voluntarily."

"I must warn you, sir, that you needn't say anything further unless you wish to do so but that anything you do say will be taken down in writing and may be given in evidence if you are charged with an offense."

"And if I refuse?"

"Then I shall get a warrant for your arrest."

"Get one if you like," said Eric. "I've committed no offense, and I'll trouble you to let me go on my way."

"Very good, sir, but I warn you that you'll be followed. So I shouldn't try to leave the country or hide. And I'll relieve you of that parcel, sir."

"You'll do nothing of the sort," said Eric. "I know my rights. It's mine."

"It's not yours, sir, as a matter of fact. It belongs to the Receiver for the Metropolitan Police, if you want to know."

The inspector opened the suitcase and took out the parcel.

"If it's any consolation to you, sir," he added, "there's no money in it. Just paper and wood. It wouldn't be much use to you, sir, but in any event, as I told you, it belongs to the Metropolitan Police. However, as you won't come to Scotland Yard, I'm going to open it in your presence. The other officer will see that nothing blows away."

Unhappily Eric watched the parcel opened and saw the wood and newspaper. All his dreams for the future had gone, but he'd now have to be pretty careful about the present. They'd put it across him if they could.

"Make a note of this, please, officer," he said.

A notebook was immediately produced.

"I never demanded anything from Mr. or Mrs. Woodthorpe," he dictated, "and I never made any threat to either of them."

The officer wrote it down.

"Would you care to sign it, sir?" he asked.

"I don't see why not," said Eric and signed the statement.

"Might we have your address, sir?"

Eric paused. He had thought of running away, but it was difficult to hide indefinitely and, if he were caught, it would look bad before a judge and jury. He gave it to them.

"Thank you, sir," said the officer. "We shall be arresting you quite soon."

"And I shall be suing you for false arrest," said Eric.

"I told you we're getting a warrant, sir. You'd have to sue the magistrate, and I think your solicitor will tell you that can't be done. I should see a solicitor, if I were you, sir. You'll need one. It's a very serious offense."

"It's not an offense at all," said Eric. "Now, kindly let me go."

10 *Solicitor and Client*

BUT, THOUGH ERIC PUT AS GOOD A FACE ON IT AS he could when speaking to the police, he was desperately worried. He tried to comfort himself by repeating over and over again in his mind that he had made no demand. "Blackmail is demanding with menaces. I've made no demand. How can they get me for it?" But in his heart he felt sure that they would. He must get legal advice.

He chose a solicitor and was soon having an interview.

"What are you being charged with?" asked the lawyer, whose name was Mandrake.

"Well, I'm not charged yet," said Eric, "but I'm sure I will be."

"What with?"

"I'm not guilty."

"I dare say, but what aren't you guilty of?"

"Well, it's absurd, but they said they were going to get a warrant."

"Look, Mr. Baines," said Mr. Mandrake, "it's expensive enough to consult a solicitor anyway, but, if you beat about the bush, it takes longer and costs more. You must tell me what it's all about."

Eventually Eric told him, and, as he did so, the solicitor's face hardened. Blackmail is not a popular crime, and soon, from the way in which Eric told the story, Mr. Mandrake could visualize the terrible anguish that Eric had inflicted on the Woodthorpes, particularly on Mary. He considered whether to take on the case or not, but eventually decided that he could not properly refuse. Every criminal was entitled to a fair trial, whatever he'd done, and he couldn't have one unless he were adequately defended.

"I can't pretend I like the case," said Mr. Mandrake, "but, if you want me to apply for legal aid for you in the Magistrate's Court, I'll do so."

"What do you mean, you don't like the case?" asked Eric, knowing very well what the solicitor meant, but feeling that he must keep his end up.

"Whether you made a demand or not, you made these people's lives hell. What d'you expect me to do? Give you a medal or something? I'll defend you as well as I can, if you want me to, but it's idle to pretend I shall enjoy it. Blackmail is an ugly word and an ugly offense."

"But I'm not guilty," protested Eric, "I demanded nothing. You don't believe me, I suppose."

"It doesn't matter whether I believe you or not. It's my job to defend you, not believe you. But, in fact, I'm quite prepared to accept what you say. You thought these people were paying you fifty thousand pounds to keep the father of the child they'd adopted out of the picture, and you say they offered the money voluntarily."

Eric brightened a little.

"Well, if you believe that, why don't you like the case?"

"If you want to know, because people wouldn't offer money like that unless they were frightened out of their wits. And who frightened them, d'you suppose?"

Eric's brightness was short-lived.

"How can you defend me if you haven't faith in me?" asked Eric.

"To tell you the truth," said Mr. Mandrake, "I'd be delighted if you'd take the case elsewhere. But having faith in a case makes no difference to me or any other competent solicitor. It's our job to do the best we can for our clients without putting up a false case for them. If we win, so much the better; if we lose, ten to one the man's guilty. No, that's wrong. A hundred to one more like."

"Then you think I'm guilty?"

"Morally, of course you are. I haven't had time to consider whether we can put up a technical legal defense. Now, d'you want me to do the case or not?"

"What'll I get if I go down?"

"Have you a record?"

"Not for this."

"But you've been convicted of other things? How often?"

"Six or seven times."

"What's the most you've had so far?"

"Eighteen months."

"Well, it depends on the charge against you. There's no actual offense called blackmail, but there are several different offenses that are all commonly called blackmail. In the worst of them you can get life."

Eric went white.

"Life?" he queried.

"Yes," said Mr. Mandrake, "life. But I don't think your offense is one of those. I shall have to look it up."

"Well, for God's sake, do so," said Eric. Life! It was a terrible thought.

The solicitor fetched a book from his shelves and turned up various pages in it.

"Quite sure you didn't write anything?" he asked.

"Absolutely," said Eric.

"Well, you didn't threaten to accuse them of a crime, that I certainly believe. No, you can't get life."

"Thank God!" said Eric.

"I don't believe you do," said Mr. Mandrake rather too quietly for Eric to make out the words. He was a churchwarden and had taken a considerable dislike to Eric. It is curious how some religious people lack compassion. However terrible the crime, however severe the punishment on the criminal should be, a man who would describe himself as a Christian should have compassion. And indeed, however much any normal person would have disliked Eric and could not humanly have avoided wishing for him the severest punishment while he was in the process of bleeding Mary, yet, when the miserable man is brought low and is squirming on the ground, it would be difficult for many people not to pity him. A strong man in adversity is a subject for pride and admiration; the bully and the coward, brought low, can still be a subject for pity.

"What can I get?" said Eric.

"I repeat, it depends what the charge is. We shall have to see. But it can't be life, anyway."

"Ten years?" guessed Eric.

"I don't know. Anything from two to fourteen years. But yours is most likely to be only a two-year offense."

"That's better," said Eric.

"I can't be sure," said Mr. Mandrake, "and I must warn you that they may put in several charges and you could be given several consecutive sentences. How many times did Mrs. Woodthorpe pay you money?"

"Six or seven."

"The same number as your convictions," commented Mr. Mandrake.

"What's that got to do with it?"

"Just a coincidence. Well, if they put on six or seven charges, the judge could give you six or seven times two years."

"Then the maximum sentence makes no difference," said Eric.

"Not if the judge thinks two years aren't enough."

"And do you think he will?"

"I should think so," said Mr. Mandrake. "If you're found guilty, it's a horrible offense, and Mrs. Woodthorpe must have suffered terribly. If you want to know my views, you shall have them. I think that two years are quite inadequate."

"That's a comfort," said Eric bitterly. "You said that as though you wanted to see me behind bars forever."

"If you want to go to another solicitor, pray do," said Mr. Mandrake. "It's not my job to comfort you but to get you off altogether if I can, or to get as small a sentence as possible if you're convicted. If you want comfort, go to your God whom you thanked not so long ago."

This time Mr. Mandrake could not control his thoughts and he spoke the words aloud.

"For all you care, I might," said Eric, thinking that he had been told to go to hell.

"Now, do you want me to appear for you or not? I shall want ten guineas if you do, but if, as I expect, you get legal aid in the Magistrate's Court, there'll be no more to pay after that. Need you'll get some back. If you're not arrested, I'll return you eight guineas. If you don't want me to act for you, I shall charge you nothing for this interview. Now, what do you want?"

In spite of his dislike for Mr. Mandrake, the solicitor's directness made Eric feel that he would defend him well. He handed over ten guineas. The next day he was arrested.

11 The Trial

MARY AND BILL WERE NOW FEELING MUCH HAP-
pier. It was true that they were not entirely out of the wood
and it was possible that Hugh's father had some rights in the
matter. But, if he had, he had himself given no sign that he
was interested in Hugh. Why not, if he was? Moreover, with
luck the blackmailer might give them the information they
wanted, if not voluntarily while in prison, at any rate in the
witness box.

In due course they attended a conference with a representative of the Director of Public Prosecutions. First of all, he assured them that they would be known as Mr. and Mrs. X, so
that the prosecution would not be likely to do them any harm.
Secondly, he said that, if the man pleaded *not guilty* and went
into the witness box, he could be asked about Hugh's father.

Altogether, it was a great relief to them both to have told
the police everything. They had handed over the responsibility.
And, as the days and weeks went by with no further calls by

frightening strangers, their confidence increased more and more. It was unpleasant having to give evidence at the Magistrate's Court, but no more than unpleasant. They were allowed to be called Mr. and Mrs. X, and the press did not bother them unduly.

Eventually Eric came up for trial at the Old Bailey. He pleaded *not guilty* and Mary and Bill had to give evidence again. Their cross-examination was no great ordeal. It was plain that the defense was the absence of threat or demand. At the close of the case for the prosecution Eric gave evidence. This was the moment for which Mary and Bill had been waiting. Eric had made no statement while awaiting trial and he said nothing about Hugh's father in his examination-in-chief. Counsel for the Crown then rose to cross-examine and Mary and Bill listened intently.

"Do you really know the father of this boy?" asked counsel.

"I think so," said Eric.

"You *think?*" said counsel. "Either you do or you don't."

"How can I *know* he was the father?" asked Eric. "I wasn't present when the boy was born."

"You're quite right," said counsel. "And even that wouldn't have told you. It was my fault. What you mean is that you have met a man who *said* he was the father?"

"Yes."

"Where did you meet him?"

Before Eric could answer, his own counsel spoke quietly to his opponent.

"Don't answer that question for the moment, Mr. Smith," said counsel. "Would Your Lordship forgive me for a moment?"

The judge nodded, and there was a whispered conversation between the two counsel. To Mary's and Bill's dismay, when they had finished, prosecuting counsel went on:

"Thank you, My Lord. Did the father ever ask you to approach Mr. or Mrs. X?" Apparently he had completely abandoned the line of questioning which would show who the father was.

"No," said Eric.

"Then why did you approach them?"

"I thought I might do them a good turn."

"A good turn?"

"Yes."

"In what way?"

"Well, I knew the father might go looking for the child."

"How did you know that?"

"From what the father said."

"And how could you help Mr. and Mrs. X?"

"By heading the father off, if he tried to find them. That's what they asked me to do. And they offered to pay me well to do it."

"How could you head the father off?"

"By telling him I hadn't found the child, or by giving him misleading information."

"By lying to him, in other words?"

"You can put it like that."

"How would you put it?"

Eric was silent.

"Well, how *would* you put it?"

"Like I said."

"You were being paid to tell lies to the father?"

"That's not illegal."

"Never mind whether it's illegal or not. That is what you say happened. You were to receive fifty thousand pounds to tell lies to the father? That's your case, isn't it?"

"I suppose so."

"Don't let's have any supposing about it. Is that not your

case—that you were to be paid fifty thousand pounds for telling lies to the father?"

"If you like. But I never asked for the fifty thousand."

"You asked for the parcel, did you not? You've heard the recording taken by the police of your last interview with Mrs. Woodthorpe—I mean Mrs. X. That was your voice asking for the parcel, wasn't it?"

"I didn't ask for it."

"You said, 'There was a parcel, wasn't there?' Didn't you?"

"You've got the recording."

"But that's what you said, isn't it?"

"Suppose it was?"

"By saying 'There was a parcel, wasn't there?' didn't you mean to ask for the parcel?"

"I just said it."

"I know, but if it wasn't asking for the parcel what did it mean? 'There was a parcel, wasn't there?' " repeated counsel. "That meant, did it not, 'Please give me the parcel which you've previously arranged to give me'?"

"You can twist anything."

"I hope I'm not but, if I am, you tell me what I'm twisting. Why did you refer to the parcel at all if it was not your object to get it?"

Eric did not answer.

"Hadn't you come to the house for the express purpose of getting the parcel?"

"Perhaps."

"For what other reason had you come? To have a glass of sherry?"

"It's easy to be sarcastic from where you are," said Eric. "You wouldn't find it so pleasant from here."

The judge did not intervene. He rather agreed with Eric.

"I'm sorry," said counsel, "but can you tell me any other

object you had in coming to the house, except to get the parcel?"

Eric was silent again.

"May I take your silence to mean that you had no other object?"

"I suppose so."

"Very well then. Having no other object in coming to the house, except to collect the parcel, what else could you have meant when you said, 'There was a parcel, wasn't there?' except 'Please give me the parcel'?"

"What am I supposed to say to that?" asked Eric.

"You're supposed to say the truth," said the judge.

"It was too long a question," said Eric. "By the time he came to the end I'd forgotten the beginning."

"Mrs. X didn't mention the parcel before you did, did she?"

"No."

"Weren't you getting a bit anxious by that time that she'd forgotten it?"

"I wasn't anxious about anything."

"Didn't you want the parcel? You'd come to get it."

"That was up to them."

"So, if Mrs. X hadn't given it to you, you'd have just gone away?"

"Certainly."

"And you wouldn't have told any lies to the father?"

"Probably wouldn't have seen him."

"So you wouldn't have said anything to him at all, true or false?"

"Most likely not."

"But, if you got the parcel, you were going—to use your own words—to head the father off?"

"Yes."

"And the way you'd head him off would be by saying something to him?"

"Yes, I've said so."

"So it comes to this, doesn't it? No parcel, no heading off. Parcel, and you tell the father something to head him off."

"Something like that."

"What did you think was in the parcel?"

Although everyone knew that the price was fifty thousand pounds, it was a horrible question for Eric to have to answer. It seemed almost impossible to answer it without looking guilty, or at least self-conscious. But it had to be done. This was a question he couldn't avoid. After a short pause:

"Fifty thousand pounds," he said.

"Are you a rich man, Mr. Smith?" asked counsel.

"Of course not," said Eric.

"Then fifty thousand pounds must seem a lot of money to you?"

"It's quite a lot."

"Had you fifty thousand shillings of your own at the time—that's twenty-five hundred pounds?"

"No."

"Perhaps you had fifty thousand pence. That's a little over two hundred pounds."

"Yes, I had."

"Where had that come from? Mr. and Mrs. X?"

"It could have."

"It could have come from anyone. But didn't it, in fact, come from them?"

"I had money of my own as well."

"I dare say. But some of your fifty thousand pence had come from Mr. and Mrs. X?"

"I expect so."

"Then, wherever it had come from, only having fifty thousand pence . . ."

"I had more than three hundred pounds."

"No doubt. How much of it from Mr. and Mrs. X?"

Eric regretted his interruption.

"I don't remember."

"Well, never mind. Having under one thousand pounds, shall we say, wasn't the prospect of getting fifty thousand a very desirable one?"

"I was prepared to accept it."

Counsel checked himself from saying that that was very magnanimous of Eric.

"So you had gone to the house to collect fifty thousand pounds in a parcel, which you were prepared to accept if it was offered to you?"

"Yes."

"And, if you got it, you'd speak to the father, and, if you didn't, you wouldn't?"

"Something of the sort."

"Why didn't you ask Mrs. X if they were still prepared to offer you fifty thousand pounds?"

"There was no need."

"Wasn't there? She said nothing about it. It was you who raised the subject with your 'There was a parcel, wasn't there?' "

"I mentioned it."

"You mentioned it because you wanted it, didn't you?"

"I didn't ask for it."

"Why did you mention it then?"

"In case she still wanted to give it to me."

"You seem very anxious that no one should think you made a demand. Are you?"

"That's what I'm charged with, isn't it? Demanding with menaces."

"Not exactly," said counsel. "But never mind about the actual charge for the moment. You've always been anxious, haven't you, that no one should be able to say you'd demanded anything?"

"Well, I haven't."

"Then, if you've a clear conscience on the subject, why did you ask Mr. X to write that piece of paper about payment being made voluntarily and all their own idea?"

"That was the truth, wasn't it?"

"Was it? All their own idea to pay you fifty thousand pounds in return for your heading off the father?"

"It meant a good deal more than that to them," said Eric incautiously.

"You mean the possible loss of their child meant more to them than fifty thousand pounds?"

"You can't value a child in money."

"I agree, but it was what you said that I was referring to. 'They valued their child at more than fifty thousand pounds,' I think you said."

"They begged me to head off the father."

"And they pressed fifty thousand pounds on you to do it?"

"Yes, they did."

"And you were prepared to accept it?"

"Why not? If they valued my work at that amount, why shouldn't I take it?"

"You didn't think you were being overpaid?"

"A lot of people are overpaid."

"Then you agree that you were being overpaid?"

"It isn't a crime."

"That's a matter for His Lordship and the jury. But do you agree that you were grossly overpaid?"

"It was a lot, I agree."

"Compared with what you had to do to earn it, it was a fantastic amount."

"It was a lot. Some people have earned a million easier."

"Oh—who?"

"No one in particular. I've read about such things."

"So you thought fifty thousand pounds was a fair amount for Mr. and Mrs. X to pay you for your services?"

"They agreed to pay it."

"Now, let's come to the first charge against you. Threatening to publish or refrain from publishing . . ."

"I didn't threaten anyone and there was never any question of publishing anything. I'm not a publisher."

"It's lawyers' language, I'm afraid," said counsel. "Publishing includes speaking or writing to a person. Threatening includes saying something to a person. You don't have to produce a mask or a revolver or even an ugly look. If I said to you, 'I will tell your employer what I know unless you give me fifty pounds and I won't tell him if you do give me fifty pounds,' that would be threatening to publish."

"Is this supposed to be a legal lecture or something?"

"Well, you've got to understand the question," said counsel. "So I'm explaining it before I ask it. The section under which the charges are laid makes it an offense for a person to threaten to publish or refrain from publishing any matter or thing about any person whether living or dead with intent to extort any property from any other person. Now you did say that whether or not you headed off the child's father depended on whether you were paid fifty thousand pounds. So you said, 'If you pay me fifty thousand pounds I will say something to the child's father and, if you don't, I won't.' "

"What am I supposed to answer to all that?"

"The effect of your conversations with Mr. and Mrs. X was that, if you were paid, you'd speak to the father, and, if you weren't, you wouldn't."

"What of it!"

"And you intended, did you not, to get fifty thousand pounds from Mr. and Mrs. X if you could?"

"I intended nothing. They offered it."

"You hoped to get fifty thousand pounds?"

"I hope to win the pools."

"Quite so. Many of us do. This was almost as good as the pools, wasn't it, and you hoped you'd get the money? All I'm asking you is—you hoped to get it, didn't you? You hoped for it?"

"I may have."

"Have you ever been in for a football pool?"

"Yes."

"Have you ever gone in for it without hoping you'd win a big prize?"

"Of course not."

"You wouldn't say about the pools that you may have hoped to win a big prize; why do you say that you *may have* hoped to get fifty thousand pounds from Mr. and Mrs. X? You hoped for it, didn't you? And I might add you hoped for it very much indeed, didn't you?"

"If they'd give it to me, yes."

"And you felt pretty confident, on the day you collected the parcel, that the fear of losing their baby would make Mr. and Mrs. X pay almost anything?"

"I didn't think about it. They offered it and I took it."

"You mean you thought you took it," said counsel, and sat down.

So the whole of the evidence had been given without Mary and Bill learning a word about the father. What had happened? They had pretty well been promised that the questions would be asked. Well, they would have to wait before they learned the answer. So they listened as patiently as they could to the

speeches of counsel and, finally, the summing-up of the judge.
Among other things he said this:

"Members of the jury, this is in one way a somewhat unusual
case. In most trials for serious offenses there is a substantial
dispute between the evidence given on behalf of the prosecution
and the defense. But in this case the prosecution's evidence is
virtually admitted. And what you have to ask yourselves is
whether what the accused did amounted to a crime. Of course,
in considering that question you will pay careful attention to
the evidence of the accused himself. In this country no man can
normally be convicted of a serious crime unless he intended to
do something wicked. If you doubt whether the accused had
any such intention, you will acquit him.

"You have heard the accused's explanation of what happened. If you have some doubt as to whether or not he was
fleecing Mr. and Mrs. X unmercifully, playing on their love
for their adopted child, you will acquit him. It is not for him
to prove his innocence but for the prosecution to prove his guilt.
The Crown has got to prove to your complete satisfaction that
this man was deliberately squeezing Mr. and Mrs. X, until out
of desperation they paid him. A good deal has been said by
the accused and his counsel about the absence of any demand.
The actual section under which the charges arise does not, in
fact, contain the word 'demand.' The two important words it
contains are 'threaten' and 'extort.' To threaten, in this context,
means simply to say or imply that you will do or refrain from
doing something which you know the person you are speaking
to will want you not to do or to do, as the case may be. To
extort means to squeeze something out of a person which is
not due from him and which he would not otherwise pay.

"No particular words are necessary to constitute a threat.
Indeed, in some cases no words at all are necessary. For ex-

ample, if with one hand a man pointed a revolver at another man's wife and with the other hand made motions to indicate that he would like some money, that would amount quite plainly to a threat to shoot the wife if the husband did not pay. Similarly, if one man knew that another man did not want something about him published in the newspapers, the mere lifting of a telephone receiver, without a word spoken, could amount to a threat to publish; and, if it were accompanied by a physical indication that money was required, it would constitute the offense with which the accused is charged.

"The question you, therefore, have to ask yourselves is: 'Was this a bona fide piece of business, albeit with a very large sum coming the way of the accused as a result, or was the accused by his visits and by what he said at those visits plainly threatening Mr. and Mrs. X with some disclosure to the father of their child if they did not pay him well?' And bear in mind that it is not for the accused to prove that this was a bona fide piece of business; it is for the prosecution to prove to your complete satisfaction that it was not. They must prove, in other words, that all this talk about no demanding and no threats, all this talk about Mr. or Mrs. X offering the money and not being asked for it, is pure eyewash, and that it is a plain and simple case of brutal blackmail. They must prove that the accused terrified Mrs. X with the thought of losing her child with the deliberate object of extracting money from her or her husband or both of them.

" 'She offered the money,' he said. 'I never asked for it.' You will consider first whether a loving mother might very well offer anything to avoid losing her child, and secondly whether an ordinary man like the accused would not know this. If you think it possible, even faintly possible, that when the accused started his chats with Mrs. X he had no guilty intention of any kind, that he was just a friendly man exchanging a few words over the garden gate with a little boy and his charming mother and that, as far as the accused was concerned, he was immensely surprised at being offered money, even the fantastic sum which he eventually came to collect, then you will acquit him.

"Members of the jury, the law is sometimes said to be an ass, and undoubtedly there is no system of law either here or abroad which does not contain serious flaws. But, as far as these offenses are concerned, you need not worry about deficiencies in the law. The word 'blackmail' does not occur in the statute book. The various offenses that are commonly called blackmail are couched in various terms. One of them is called 'demanding with menaces.' There is more to it than that, but that is not the section under which the accused is charged, and those words are enough for my purpose. Do you think the accused was perhaps aware—if only vaguely—that 'demanding with menaces' could be an offense? Is that why he made his statement to the police when he was stopped with the parcel, and why he asked Mr. X to write on the piece of paper that was found on him when arrested? Be that as it may, in this case all you have in effect to consider, members of the jury, is whether this is a plain case of blackmail, as plain as you can have, or whether there is some doubt about it. If there is any doubt about it, you will acquit the accused; but, if not, you will convict him. There are four similar charges against him. I personally cannot see any reason for differentiating between them. If you convict or acquit on one, in my opinion you should convict or acquit on all. Perhaps you would like to retire."

The jury retired but returned in ten minutes with a verdict of guilty. It was then disclosed that Eric had several previous convictions for comparatively trivial crimes and had been sent to prison on two occasions. Mary and Bill then learned why prosecuting counsel had not persisted with his questions about Hugh's father.

"My Lord," said counsel, "my learned friend told me in the middle of my cross-examination that the accused had met this child's father in prison. Accordingly, I did not proceed with my questions, lest the fact that the accused had been to prison might become known to the jury."

"Very proper," said the judge.

"There is one matter, however," went on counsel, "which I should like to mention to Your Lordship. As you may imagine, both Mr. and Mrs. X have suffered the greatest distress as a result of the accused's behavior. They are now left in a state of complete uncertainty. Has the accused ever met the father? Does the father intend to take steps to try to set aside the adoption order? And so on. Naturally, no question has been asked of the accused since his arrest on these matters. It occurs to me, however, that he could in a very slight way atone for the distress he has caused Mr. and Mrs. X, by giving this information now."

"I see," said the judge. "I shall postpone sentence on the accused until next session. He has heard what you have said and can act upon it or not, as he and his advisers think fit. It would not, however, be fair of me to allow this to happen without saying that I consider this to be one of the worst cases of blackmail which it has been my misfortune to hear and that, in my opinion, the maximum sentence for each of the offenses with which the accused is charged is far too little for this particular case."

12 Eric's Story

FOR BILL AND MARY THE POSSIBILITY THAT HUGH
was the son of a man serving a prison sentence was a great
shock. What Eric had said was not necessarily true, but the way
in which the statement had come to be made had the semblance
of truth. Nor could they think of any reason for Eric's telling
his counsel that the boy's father was in prison, if it were not
true. The mother had said that he was a solicitor. That could
still be true. He might no longer be a solicitor or he might have
been sent to prison for a motoring offense. Once again it was
the not knowing which was most disturbing. The mother might
have been lying altogether. The father could be a hardened
criminal, with a record for violence or fraud, or someone like
Eric. Whatever he was, they would love Hugh none the less
and want him just as much. But it was terribly worrying not to
know. More particularly for Mary.

"It's environment that counts," Bill said to her. "Hugh's
been with us ever since he was under eighteen months. There's
nothing wrong with his progress."

"But you wouldn't expect him to show criminal tendencies yet," said Mary, always ready now to torture herself.

"He's not going to show any criminal tendencies," said Bill, "at any time. If he does, it'll be entirely your fault. In any event, we still don't know for certain who his father is. I wonder if that fellow will talk. I'm afraid the judge gave a pretty clear indication that he'd get the maximum sentence, in any event. I suppose it wouldn't be fair not to, but it's not much help to us."

Meanwhile, Eric was having a conversation on the same subject in Brixton prison with Mr. Mandrake.

"Why should I tell them anything?" he asked sulkily.

"You've nothing to lose, have you?" said Mr. Mandrake. "And you might gain something, though I must admit that's a bit doubtful."

"As a matter of fact," said Eric, "there's very little I can tell. I could make something up, of course."

"No doubt," said Mr. Mandrake, "but I'm not interested in that. If you've anything to say, I want the truth."

"But how will you know if it's the truth?"

"I shan't."

"Then it doesn't matter what I tell you."

"Mr. Baines, or Mr. Smith, whichever you prefer to be called," said Mr. Mandrake, "I am not prepared to argue about the way in which we carry on the legal profession. Kindly tell me what you know, or say you won't."

"There's very little, really."

"So you said before," said Mr. Mandrake, and reached for his hat.

"All right," said Eric, "I'll tell you, but I'm frightened that it's not enough to help."

"Let me be the judge of that," said Mr. Mandrake.

"Well, it was interview day at the Scrubs. My girl friend came to see me, but we ran out of things to say. There you are—only fifteen minutes to go, and you can't think of a bleeding thing to say. You don't know what prison's like. And now I'm going for ten years and you don't care," he said bitterly.

"What happened on interview day?" asked Mr. Mandrake calmly.

"Well, there was this chap next to me seeing his wife or his girl, I didn't know which at the time. I thought it was his wife. She was quite smartly dressed. I reckoned there'd be some money there."

"Well?"

"While I was waiting for my girl friend to say something, I got listening to them and I heard her say she was moving and I took a note of the address, in my mind, of course. I wrote it down later."

"Why?"

"Well, I thought I might get a bit off her. I'd been in the same place as her husband, I might do a bit of sob-stuff. And then I heard them talking about the boy. He was obviously nuts about him, kept on asking about him. Often the same questions. And she showed him photographs. Then my girl friend said something and I didn't hear for a bit. Then just before the end I heard them again. They were still talking about the boy."

"What was the man in for?"

"Manslaughter."

"A motorcar case?"

"Goodness, no. A small boy. He was charged with murder but the jury said manslaughter. Ten years he got. They didn't like him at the Scrubs."

"Who didn't?"

"The other chaps. They don't like that sort of thing, killing kids."

"Well, what happened?"

"I came out soon afterward. And eventually I paid a call on Mrs. West, as she called herself. I told her where I came from, and, as I thought, the fact that I'd been near her husband made her listen. She gave me a cup of tea. That was a beginning, but I thought I could do better than that. A fiver, or something, I thought. And then it happened. I asked after the boy. 'What boy?' she asked. But she'd gone white and I could tell she was lying. That put ideas into my head. I went on at her. She told me to go. I got up very politely and was about to leave when I just mentioned casually that I should write to the man about there being no child. That shook her. I made as if to go out but she pulled me back. 'No,' she said. 'You mustn't.' 'How d'you spell mustn't?' I said. She reached for her bag. That suddenly gave me an idea. 'Where is the boy?' I asked. She wouldn't tell me at first. Said she didn't know. So I got up again. She burst into tears. So there I was getting somewhere. Eventually, she admitted that she was not married to the father and that she'd had the boy adopted. I forced the address out of her."

"I wonder how she knew it," said Mr. Mandrake. "She shouldn't have. Or perhaps it wasn't a serial number."

"What's all that in aid of?" asked Eric.

"It doesn't matter," said Mr. Mandrake. "You got the address from her and that's how it all started?"

"More or less," said Eric.

"Well," said Mr. Mandrake, "I don't think Mr. and Mrs. Woodthorpe are going to be very pleased with this information, but it sounds to me as though you're telling the truth. Did you have any money from Mrs. West?"

"Certainly not," said Eric virtuously.

"Well, you blackmailed her into giving you the information to enable you to blackmail someone else. Not a very pretty picture. That wouldn't reduce your sentence much."

"You're not going to tell all this?" said Eric, somewhat aghast.

"Fortunately for you, I don't have to. If you agree, I'll simply tell them that you met the father in prison, called on the mother, found that they were not married, and got the child's address from her. I'll also say what the father is in for, though they won't thank me for that bit. Still, I'd better tell them."

When counsel learned of this information they asked to see the judge privately.

"We've got a very difficult problem, Judge," said prosecuting counsel, "and I wonder if you could help us. I couldn't think of a solution myself."

"Certainly, if I can," said the judge.

"We've found out who the father of the boy is, that's if Smith is telling the truth, and it sounds as if he is."

"Well?"

"He's doing ten years for assaulting a boy and killing him. Now, have I got to tell that to the adopters? It'd drive the woman round the bend."

"Well, you're not her counsel," said the judge. "I don't see why you should. And, even if you were, I'm not at all sure that she should be told. What a dreadful story. After all they've gone through, and then to be told what the father's like."

"But what are we to say, Judge? The case was adjourned for Smith to give information. Now he's given it. What's to be said in Court and outside it? We can't lie about it, can we?"

"No, certainly not," said the judge.

"Well then, Judge," said counsel, "suppose all that's said in Court is that Smith has given all the information he can. The Woodthorpes are bound to ask what it was when the case is over. If we refuse to tell them, they'll be wondering all the time what it is, and if we tell them, it will be just as bad or worse."

The judge thought for a little time.

"The only suggestion I can make is that you tell them that the man is in prison for ten years for manslaughter, and, if they ask any more, you say that I don't think they ought to be given more details of another man's conviction."

"Supposing they ask me point-blank—do I know all those details?"

"You can say 'Yes,' but that you propose to abide by what I've said. I don't pretend it's a perfect solution. It's rather like a doctor when his patient oughtn't to be told he's got cancer. He doesn't want to lie and tries to find a way round it. Well, that's the only way I can think of. It tells them a good deal but doesn't give them the final blow."

13 More Conferences

WHEN MARY AND BILL HEARD THAT HUGH'S
father might be serving a ten-year sentence for manslaughter,
they were horrified but, of course, they wanted to know more.
What sort of manslaughter was it? Ten years suggested near-
murder. Was it a crime of passion, or what? Was West a solicitor? They were simply not told, and even Eric could not
have said if West had been a solicitor or what he was.

Before passing sentence, the judge had intended to ask Eric
if he had given all the information in his possession, but in the
circumstances he refrained.

"Eric Smith," he said, "I believe that you have done what you
can to help and, though this is not a case which calls for the
least clemency—indeed, as I said before, it is the worst case of
its kind I have ever heard—nevertheless, you have given some
information, and this will be reflected in my sentence. You will
go to prison on each of the first three counts for two years and
on the fourth count for ten months. The sentences will run

consecutively. That will mean six years and ten months in all."

It was no less than Eric had expected, and he had got two months off. But he was hardly grateful to Mr. Mandrake for his advice. The time for gratitude would come toward the end. A man facing a sentence of nearly seven years takes little comfort from the fact that it is not quite seven years. Eric went to the cells a sadder man, but little wiser.

Mary and Bill were glad to see him go, but not out of revenge. Neither of them was the sort of person to want revenge, except possibly for a very short time. But they were relieved that he would not trouble them any more. As for the future, they were left in a state of complete uncertainty and so they went again to Mr. Luttrell and told him what had happened.

"It sounds as though he was speaking the truth," said Mr. Luttrell, "and I can only tell you what the possibilities are on the basis that he is. If he isn't, we have absolutely no knowledge of what the truth is and it would be impossible to make the faintest guess as to what may happen. But, if what he said is true, it does mean, I'm afraid, that there is a man in prison who is unaware—unless he has since been told—that his child is no longer at the house where he left it. Now, don't be too alarmed," he added, as he saw Mary's face pale. "If we have been told the truth, the father and mother are not married. And, if that's so, not only is the father's consent not required, but, as I think I told you before, he has no right whatever in the matter, unless he is liable under an order or agreement to pay maintenance."

"But how can we tell whether he is or he isn't?" asked Bill. "Should we try to find out?"

"On the whole, I think not," said Mr. Luttrell. "That might very well stir things up. In any event, it would not improve your chance of keeping the child."

"Improve our chance," said Mary almost desperately. "D'you

mean that we have a good chance of losing him? We can't. We won't. You must prevent it."

"If we do nothing, we shall never know what to expect or how to prepare for it," said Bill. "For example, if we knew there was likely to be trouble, we could go and live abroad. We shouldn't hesitate if there was danger of losing Hugh."

Mary looked gratefully at Bill.

"But naturally we don't want to do anything so radical unless it's absolutely necessary. It would be a complete upheaval and I'd have to consider the financial position. But if we knew that there was a real danger of our losing the boy, we'd want to make preparations. And the longer we had, the better."

"That's true," said Mr. Luttrell, "but consider this aspect. The man will very likely never know about the child until he leaves prison. That might not be for years. The child will be nine in, say, five years. If you then decided to go abroad, it would only have to be for about seven years. If you stir things up now, the man could start proceedings now, and you might have to go abroad for twelve years. Besides, as I've told you, it's very likely that he has no rights at all. It doesn't sound as though there was an affiliation order. If there wasn't an order, why should there be an agreement? It's quite true that the agreement doesn't have to be in writing, but, if the parties were living together, why should they have made an agreement?"

"Very easy to invent," said Bill. "If they both said there was one, what chance would we have?"

"There's no sign whatever that the mother's interested in the matter. She parted willingly with the child and has never made a move since. She doesn't want the child, obviously. In any event, you must remember that, if the worst came to the worst, and if the father could prove that there was an agreement for him to maintain the child, he is only entitled to be heard by the Court in the matter. And, when he was heard, what on earth could he say to make the Court upset the order? Here is a man who has an illegitimate child and then goes to prison. The child is in a happy home and has been for two years. What judge in his senses would take the child away from that home, whatever the father said? It would only be if the boy was his legitimate child that there could be real trouble. Then I agree that there could be. But there is no father named on the birth certificate. So the chances of the man having the rights of a legitimate father are minimal."

"So, you mean that whatever happens, unless Hugh is legitimate, we can't lose him?" said Mary, rather more happily.

"I think I can fairly say that," said Mr. Luttrell. "I can't see how any Court could take that child away from you, unless it had to do so. And the only circumstances in which it might have to do so would be if he were legitimate."

"But even then," said Bill, "the welfare of the child would come first, surely? And, as you said, no sane man could take Hugh away from his happy home and hand him over to an ex-jailbird."

"That isn't quite so," said Mr. Luttrell. "The present law is that an adoption order cannot be made without the consent of both legitimate parents, unless that consent is unreasonably withheld, or unless the child has been abandoned or neglected by its parents. Now, suppose this husband—because I'm assuming for this purpose that they were married—suppose this husband, living happily with his wife and child, is suddenly taken off to prison. The wife then puts the child out for adoption. The husband knows nothing of this. He would have the right to have the order set aside, and to refuse his consent to a fresh order being made. Unless the Court held that he was being unreasonable, it would have to allow his objection, even though it thought that it would be better for the boy to stay where he was."

"We'll go abroad," said Mary.

"Mrs. Woodthorpe," said Mr. Luttrell, "you're forgetting that this is *not* a husband. That is to say, it is in the highest degree improbable that he is a husband. And, unless he's a husband and Hugh his legitimate son, in my considered opinion, although it would of course be distressing for you to have fresh proceedings and to have the matter hanging over your head, there would be no real chance of your losing the child."

"How can you be so sure he isn't a husband?" asked Mary.

"Well, Mrs. Woodthorpe," said Mr. Luttrell, "in the whole course of my career I have never yet seen a birth certificate with no father's name filled in where the child was legitimate. It stands to reason. No one would deliberately bastardize a child in that way. No sane person, anyway."

"What about a mother who hated her husband and hated the child?" asked Mary. "She might do it, mightn't she? She loathes her husband, she doesn't want children, she finds herself in the family way, is frightened of an abortion. It would be quite possible, wouldn't it, for her to run away, resume her maiden name and pretend she was just another unmarried mother?"

"To gain what?"

"To revenge herself on the wretched child. There are these strange people in the world."

"I'm surprised," said Mr. Luttrell, "that anyone so devoted to children as you are, Mrs. Woodthorpe, could even imagine the existence of such a creature. It is possible, I agree, but it's not a possibility we need consider. It's far too remote."

"If that's right," said Bill, "then we've nothing to fear. The worst that can happen is that the father can make himself a bit of a nuisance, but nothing more."

"That's my opinion," said Mr. Luttrell.

"Forgive my mentioning it again," said Bill, "but, before we went to Court for the adoption order, we came to you, and I think you now agree that you were wrong in advising us to take a short cut. If Judge Hazlewell had dealt with the mother, probably the mother would have confessed the truth, the father would have been found and the whole problem dealt with then. Then there could have been no blackmail and no anxiety now."

"That is so," said Mr. Luttrell. "I've told you I'm sorry, but the chance was such a small one, I thought it worth taking."

"But, in fact, it wasn't," said Bill, "as we now know. I have to make up my mind on the terribly important question whether we should go abroad or not. You've given your opinion. It was wrong the first time. May it not be wrong now?"

"Of course," said Mr. Luttrell, "it could be wrong. We can all be wrong. And, even when we're right, a judge can say we're wrong. There *is* no certainty in human affairs. If you're worried about the matter, I suggest you take a further opinion. Or, if you liked, we could go to counsel about it."

"And he might be wrong?"

"Of course. But if he confirmed my opinion you could feel that much more confident. And I take it that's one of the reasons you're consulting me now. To relieve yourselves of anxiety as far as is possible. If that's so, the more opinions that are the same as mine, the less anxiety."

"But, if they weren't the same as yours, the more anxiety?"

"That's true."

"What would you do in my place, Mr. Luttrell?"

"Nothing."

"You wouldn't go abroad?"

"Shouldn't dream of it."

"Well," said Bill, "my wife and I will talk it over and let you know if we want any more help. Thank you for seeing us."

On the way home from the solicitor, Mary and Bill both thought to themselves for a bit. Bill spoke first:

"Darling, I'll do whatever you want, but personally I think he's right."

"I certainly don't want to uproot ourselves if it isn't necessary and, apart from that, it wouldn't be fair to you."

"Don't worry about that. Everything's fair to me that I want. All I want is for you to be happy, you and Hugh."

"What about his suggestion of getting another opinion?"

"More legal waffle if you ask me. 'On the one hand there is this. On the other hand there is that. My opinion is this, unless the judge may think something else. On the whole the risk is small but, of course, there *is* a risk. Not a large one. If the father turns up, nothing will happen—at least, probably not. Of course, it might. One can never be sure.' And so on, and so on. I'm getting quite good at it myself."

"You are," said Mary. "That might have been Mr. Luttrell."

Part Two

14 The Other Side of the Picture

AS THE MONTHS WENT BY AND NOTHING HAP-
pened, Mary gradually ceased to worry. Occasionally she had a
terrible nightmare, but she was soon comforted when she woke
up by the sure knowledge that Hugh was in the next room. And
what a wonderful boy he was, even though his father may have
been a criminal. Life became as happy for Mary and Bill as it
was immediately after the adoption order had been made.

All this time Hugh's real father, Randolph West, was in
prison, waiting as patiently as he could for the great day of his
release to arrive, when, as he fondly thought, he would be re-
united with Hugh. The one thing that had kept him relatively
sane during his imprisonment was his love for his son. Fathers
vary. Some, like Bill, are fond of their sons and will do all in
their power to help them, but do not have the intense love of a
woman for her child. But some fathers are very like women in
their deep devotion to their children. Randolph West was a

father of this kind, and from the moment he started to serve his sentence he concentrated on his son.

At first he lived on his memories. He had not been in England when the child was born, and it was not until after he had seen the child on his return, about two months after the child's birth, that he suddenly realized that he loved the mother and adored the child. Over and over again he thought about all that happened during Hugh's first year. Even the most trivial events. The first smile that was not a smile but only wind, and the first real smile. The teeth that never seemed to come and the ones that appeared as if by magic overnight. How he had gloated at first because Hugh spoke to him before his mother, until he was told that da-da is the first childish sound and would be used by a child equally to a gorilla as to its father and mother. The inoculations and vaccination. Hugh was wonderful with them all. One year. Yet so much had happened. Over and over again he thought about it. He asked for a book from the prison library. It was Dr. Spock's *Baby and Child Care*. It was not much in demand in prison.

After a time he began to think of the future and to watch Hugh grow up at a distance. Here Dr. Spock was most helpful and enabled him to visualize what might be happening to his little son. Sometimes he took fright as a result of something which he read, and he wrote to the mother as soon as he could, begging her to take care. To provide for this and to avoid that. And in no circumstances to be afraid to call the doctor.

It was odd that a putative father should be so fond of his son. But the father was not as putative as the mother had made out to the adoption society. It was true that they had met at a dance, and that Hugh was on the way shortly after the National Anthem had been played. But, from a month after Hugh's birth, they had lived together and become fond of each other. It was the wrong way round but that wouldn't have mattered so much if they had been able to marry. Unfortunately, Randolph was already married. His wife had left him, whether for another man he did not know for certain. But she had only been apart from him for under a year when Hugh was born, so that a divorce was impossible at the time. But Randolph and Eleanor intended to marry as soon as they could.

Eleanor Parton, Hugh's mother, was twenty-seven when she had met Randolph at the dance. He had attracted her physically, as she had attracted him, but it was only after the baby's birth that a firm attachment had begun to develop. Randolph paid for all the expenses of Hugh's birth, but he did not start to live with Eleanor until after the boy had been born. He had come back from a business trip and went at once to see the two of them.

It took him quite by surprise. As soon as he saw them both together, his whole outlook changed. This was his son. But not just his. Eleanor must share the credit. After his first unsuccessful, childless marriage, he had never considered the possibility of ever having a home and a family. Then suddenly he *was* a family. Eleanor and Hugh and he. A completely new sensation surged through him. Stout Balboa may have had much the same feeling when he stared at the Pacific. It was a new world and he realized it within a minute.

Fearfully he had picked up the baby and looked at it tenderly. He said nothing and then handed it back to Eleanor. She smiled at him, but nothing was said for a full five minutes. Then he said:

"I want to come and live with you, if I shan't be in the way."

"Darling," she said, and kissed him.

"He's wonderful," said Randolph. "Why haven't we done this before?"

"Well," said Margaret, "you can't say we wasted any time. When will you come?"

"I'm here," he said. "I'm staying, if I may."

They had eleven happy months together. They were beginning to look forward to the day when they could get married and they decided to wait till then before Hugh was christened. And then came the tragedy when Randolph was arrested and charged.

He had given a lift to a small boy whom he had found walking alone on a main road and taken him to the local police station. A week later the boy had been found sexually assaulted and dead. By what were, according to Randolph, a series of horrible coincidences but, according to the police, natural links in the chain of evidence, it looked as though Randolph were the man. The matter was clinched when a few strands of material that could only have come from the boy's underclothing were proved to have been found on Randolph's coat. Everything else he could explain by coincidence, but not the strands. He said that he had only met the boy once when he gave him a lift. On that occasion it was physically impossible for any of the strands to have got onto his coat. His only explanation was that either the laboratory technicians or the police had framed him. There was absolutely no reason why they should do this. The jury were puzzled by the case. They were impressed by Randolph's denials, but they could not get over the strands and they did not believe that the police would frame Randolph. He was a perfectly respectable man and the policemen concerned had never met him before. Having regard to the way death took place, the judge just left it open to the jury to bring in a verdict of manslaughter, and this they did. It was a compromise verdict, some of the jury not being prepared to find Randolph guilty of murder. The judge sentenced him to ten years' imprisonment. With good conduct the ten years would be reduced to seven. He appealed from the verdict but with no success.

Eleanor despaired. She tried to believe in Randolph's innocence and always told him that she did. But deep down inside her she had a dreadful fear that he was guilty. Juries do not like convicting respectable people of grave crimes and they acquit if they can. He made a good impression in the witness box. Yet they convicted him. At the least, he *might* be guilty. At the worst, he was. While she was with him she assured him so apparently wholeheartedly of her belief in him that she almost convinced herself. But, as soon as she left him, those dreadful gnawing doubts returned. And then other things came into her mind. His passionate love for his son. There was no doubt of this. But might it not be the product of a warped mind which from time to time could not control pure physical passion? There was no doubt of his gentleness with Hugh when they were together. But that, she had read, was quite possible with a man who might murder another boy. Besides, Hugh was under two when Randolph was arrested. He was a schizophrenic, perhaps. At times his dear, dear self, and at others a raving lunatic. What was she to do?

Even if he were innocent, he would remain in prison for nearly seven years and, when he came out, he would be a disgraced man looking for some kind of job. He had been an important man in the business world. Who would want to be associated with him now? Even those who might possibly believe in his innocence would be afraid of what other people would think. And how could he live socially? Mothers would clutch their children in fear of him, if they knew who he was.

And what about Hugh? He would go to school while Randolph was in prison.

"What's your father do?"

"Well, at the moment he's doing seven years." What an outlook. And then, when he came out, Hugh would be about the age of the boy who was murdered. Could she bear to leave them alone together? Randolph's love for Hugh was genuine beyond question. It was the great thing in his life. But who can account for the ways of maniacs? And how could anyone tell whether he was one or not?

And then another horrible thought crossed her mind. When Hugh eventually learned the truth about his father, what would he feel? Would he believe in his innocence or be ashamed of him? No one could tell. But, whether or not Hugh could be persuaded to believe in his father, the outlook for them was a ghastly one, if not actually dangerous.

She thought about her problem for many torturing days. She, too, dearly loved her son, but in the end she made up her mind. She must put Hugh out for his adoption. It was a terrible decision for her to make, but she had to consider Hugh first. It was the only thing to do. Once she had made the decision, she moved to another neighborhood, resumed her maiden name of Parton (she had been living with Randolph as Mrs. West), and took Hugh to the adoption society.

It was not altogether surprising that, to cover her emotion, she affected an air of indifference which produced the secretary's remark about not treating the place as a cloakroom. She knew that Randolph would never consent and so she lied about his identity and their relationship. She was surprised how easy it was. From the way in which the story of her dance with a solicitor was accepted from the beginning, she wondered if a lot of little bastards were not the sons of dancing solicitors. She said that the father was a solicitor so as to attract as good a home as possible for Hugh. She felt sure that to some extent adoption societies sent children to appropriate homes. She was told the sort of people Mary and Bill were, and was pleased with what she was told.

It was terrible to part with the boy but she felt sure that she must let him go. She already owed him enough for having him at all when she was unmarried, but to impose this extra burden on him seemed to her so grossly unfair that she would have been ashamed of herself for the rest of her life if she allowed him to bear it.

She tried to console herself by imagining how dreadful it would have been not only for Hugh but for her too if she had kept him. After she had consented to the adoption order, she kept on saying to herself: "I know I'm doing right. I know I'm doing right." And, when she knew that the order was actually made, she walked for miles in the streets hardly seeing or hearing anything, but looking straight in front of her. Every now and then she said aloud: "It must have been right. It must have been right."

Eleanor now had the problem of dealing with Randolph. She had made up her mind not to tell him until almost the last possible moment. She knew how he adored Hugh and that life in prison, difficult enough as it was, would become insupportable if he knew that Hugh was gone. She replied to his letters by telling fairly simple lies. She made an excuse for not bringing Hugh to see him on her first visit, but on the second visit she told Randolph that she felt that the child shouldn't be brought into the prison. He was over a year old, was starting to talk quite a lot, and who knows what might be stirred up in his memory, however unconsciously? To Randolph's argument that the boy would have to know sometime, she replied that they'd deal with that problem when it arose. Meanwhile, she said, it would not be good for a child as it grew from one to six to be making regular visits to its father in prison. It would have to stop soon. Better not to start. Eventually, Randolph reluctantly agreed.

But it seemed that the less the father saw of the son the more he thought about him. His letters were almost entirely about

Hugh. And Eleanor had to reply. She found it very difficult at first, inventing things which she thought would please Randolph. And then he started to use Dr. Spock.

"I hope you don't let Hugh crawl round the kitchen while you're cooking," he wrote. "He might get burned from a spluttering frying pan, or you might trip and spill something on him. Dr. Spock is very strong on this."

"Don't worry," she answered. "I'm very careful about that sort of thing."

Sometimes she actually felt as though Hugh were with her, as she wrote about him to Randolph.

As time went on, it was plain that Randolph was working right through Dr. Spock. So Eleanor bought a copy too. From then on she was able to keep up with Randolph, and they each wrote long and, to Eleanor, heart-rending letters about the child who, as far as they were concerned, no longer existed.

The boy grew and grew, spoke more and more, and became a real person. Eleanor had to invent his likes and dislikes, his toys, his lessons, his progress generally. Randolph read Eleanor's news avidly. And then, when she saw him on visiting days, he asked question after question about his son. At first Eleanor had been a little embarrassed at these interviews, but soon she hardly felt she was telling a lie. The phantom world in which Hugh lived and grew seemed almost real to her.

"D'you know," she would say, "the other day he used a most extraordinary word. For a boy of his age, I mean. He must have heard me use it or something. He actually said that a picture I showed him was embarrassing. Can you believe it? Embarrassing! What'll he say next, I wonder?"

Randolph laughed.

"You'll have to be careful what *you* say," he said, "or he may come out with worse than that."

"I'll be careful," said Eleanor. "Oh—and another thing, he made you a daisy chain. And one for me too. It didn't last long enough for me to bring to show you."

The most difficult problem Eleanor had was with photographs. At first she made excuses but that could not go on indefinitely. Eventually she found a child of about the right age that lived near her, and took photographs of him. For a long time they were taken from such an angle that the face could not be clearly seen. Then very cleverly she gradually introduced bad photographs with the face blurred, until eventually Randolph became accustomed to the look of the child. Finally, she risked better photographs, and it worked.

"I don't know whether he's more like you, or me," said Randolph once. "What d'you think, darling?"

"There's nothing in it," said Eleanor. "He's got your eyes and my nose. Heaven knows where his hair comes from."

For nearly two years this terrible game went on. Hugh was now three and had settled down very happily with Mary and Bill. Eleanor started to call herself Mrs. West again, though she kept Miss Parton for business. Although Randolph was not due for release for nearly five years, Eleanor now began to wonder how and when to tell the truth to him. It would be an appalling moment. She was deeply fond of him but she was frightened too. Sometimes she thought of the details which she had given him about Hugh. What would his reaction be when he learned of the calculated deception practiced on him? Would he go mad and kill himself? Or would he kill her first? She knew that Randolph was not normally a violent or ill-tempered person. But, if he was the maniac she had almost come to believe, what would such a shock produce in the quietest of men? For seven years he would have been living with the one great hope uppermost in his mind; no, not just uppermost, filling al-

most his entire mind. First it must have been: how is my son?
And then as the months and years went by: I shall see my son
in four years. In three. In two. In one. Very soon we shall be
together again. And the last year would go slowly. With days
painfully ticked off. And then would come the night before. No
sleep for him that night. Tomorrow I shall see my son. Tomorrow. Life will begin again. At that stage he would probably
not think so much of the difficulties. Of the fact that the boy
would not know him by sight. But he would. Eleanor would
have kept his photograph constantly before the boy and spoken
of him too. No, he wouldn't be at all a stranger. And the boy
to him would be as if they'd never been parted. All the hard-
ship of the past years would disappear. He would be with his
son.

When Eleanor started thinking on these lines—and she knew
that there was no exaggeration about it—she sometimes grew
desperately afraid. Had she been right to feed him with Hugh
during all these years? Was it fair? And yet, if she had not done
so, prison would have been quite intolerable.

She had confided in no one. Then one day she decided that
she must talk to someone or burst. She had a job as secretary
with a firm of solicitors, and was on good terms with one of the
junior partners. He was unmarried and becoming fond of her.
She knew that she shouldn't have let him. When he had first
taken her out to dinner and had looked at her ring finger, he
had said:

"You've never been married?"

"What an odd question."

"Well, I know you're Miss Parton. But some girls who've
divorced their husbands go back to their maiden name."

"No," she said, "I haven't divorced my husband."

"Then you are married?" he asked.

She had hesitated for a moment. A woman can see three

moves ahead, while a man is still wondering about the first. Three moves ahead? She often sees the lot. Right up to the first check. Sometimes up to checkmate. She knew that this young man could become fond of her. She liked him and, while she had every intention of joining up with Randolph when he came out of prison, it was a great temptation to a young woman to have someone to be fond of while she was alone.

"No, I'm not married." And then she felt she must add: "Not exactly."

"Oh," he said, and there was an uncomfortable silence. "Forgive me," he went on, "I know it's not my business, but why don't you marry him?"

She could have told him that he was right, it was not his business. But, in a way, it was. It was perfectly reasonable for a young man to want to know where he stood before becoming associated with a young woman. And, anyway, he was much too nice to snub.

"He's not available at the moment."

"I see. A divorce going on?"

"Not at present."

"Hasn't done the three years yet, I suppose?" he said.

"Only two," said Eleanor.

"Oh well," said the young man, "if you don't mind going out to dinner with me in the circumstances, I hope you'll come again. I'm not married and never have been."

So she had started going out with Jeremy Norton. And he was kind and gentle and understanding. Not the sort of solicitor who slips away with you after the National Anthem and disappears. She realized that he was falling in love with her, but she was much too weak to send him away. The burden of Hugh and Randolph was so great that she needed this outlet. She knew it was unfair and that, when Randolph came out of prison, the young man would be left with only her grateful thanks. But he was grown up. He was a lawyer. One must have something in life except a burden. His heart would get whole again. You can be utterly miserable for a time in youth when the loved one goes off with someone else, but it takes two to make love, and a heart that has not been loved cannot be broken. So she told herself. Meanwhile, Jeremy provided her only source of happiness while Randolph was away.

And then after two years, when thoughts of Randolph coming out started to weigh on her, she felt she must tell Jeremy. She must have help from someone. And she was lucky in her choice. The best type of human love is everything St. Paul said it is. And in Jeremy's case it was full of kindness, compassion and unselfishness.

"I want your help," she began, on the evening she told him.

"Of course," he said. "Anything. Anything at all. You know."

"I know," she said, "and I oughtn't to ask you. You of all people. When I'm going to hurt you beyond measure. But I need help so terribly."

"There's nothing I wouldn't do for you."

"That's what makes me feel so awful."

"Tell me."

Eventually, after false starts and pauses, she told him. As she did so, he looked at her with such compassion that she had to ask him not to.

"I can't stand it," she said. "You're so good and kind."

He looked away.

"I'm sorry," he said. "I know I oughtn't to be so fond of you. But I'm so glad I am. So happy. All I want to do now is to help."

She took his hand and pressed it.

After a little she said:

"What should I do? What can I do? To tell him now would
be terrible. To tell him later may be worse. I just don't know.
I could really kill myself to get out of it all."

"You mustn't think of it."

"I won't. I promise," she said. "But d'you know why not?"

"Well?"

"It'll sound awfully silly. And in some ways I think it's
dreadful of me. But d'you know . . ."

She paused so long that he said:

"Go on. Tell me."

"It's just ridiculous. It isn't really me. It's another part of
me. But . . . but . . . I want to know how it ends."

He smiled.

"Isn't that terrible?" she said. "This awful problem. The
dreadful shock Randolph is going to have. Is he mad? Now,
mightn't it drive him mad? Anything might happen. And yet
something in me—something quite outside myself—wants to
know what *is* going to happen."

"A lot of people live for just that reason," said Jeremy. "They
don't like going out in the middle. It's quite natural. Man's such
an inquisitive animal. Almost from the time he's born."

"I know all about that," said Mary, smiling slightly. "Dr.
Spock has a lot about it."

He laughed.

"It would be funny if it wasn't tragic," he said. "Both of you
doing your homework like that."

"I can even laugh sometimes," she said. "When I see what
page he's got to and decide which bit I shall use next. I've
actually laughed out loud, and then cried almost louder."

"We're so inquisitive that we can't bother about the things
we know about, as long as there's something else to explore.
Hunger, misery and distress are commonplace. No need to in-

vestigate them. Spend millions of pounds on getting to the moon instead. Much more exciting than feeding or clothing people. That's old hat."

"How right you are," she said. "You're such a wonderful man."

"Not in the least," he said. "And there are, of course, two sides to the question. On the face of it, it does look pretty dreadful trying to get to the moon while people are dying of hunger and disease. But, on the other hand, in the course of getting to the moon they may learn unspeakable methods of blotting out half the earth. So long as both sides know how to blot out the other, there's a chance neither will try, but, if only one side knows, it could successfully say: 'Stand and deliver.' So there you are. Going to the moon may be part of the race for survival. But I'm sorry. This is nothing to do with your problem."

"But it's nice to think that there are bigger problems than mine. I'm not important."

"Everyone's important," he said. "And you're very important to me. Now, let me think."

He thought for several minutes.

"I can only think of one solution," he said, "and I can't pretend I think very much of it, but it may be best. I agree that you can't stop now. If a man is going to have a serious operation, the surgeon will try to do it in the most favorable circumstances. In some cases they'll wait for a few weeks to get the patient into the best possible state of health. In other words, they want him to undergo the shock to the system in optimum conditions. Well now, no one could say that a man who received a shock like this in prison would be receiving it in optimum conditions. At least, when he's out of prison, he'll have you to comfort him, you to talk to. In prison he'll probably have no one. I think you were absolutely right to do what you did. I don't think he should be told until he's actually released."

"But where? At the prison gate? On the way home? And how? How could I actually get the words out?"

He did not answer at once.

Then, "I'll tell you what," he said. "I would meet him if you liked, and tell him."

"You?" she said.

"Yes. It would be quite easy for me. Or certainly easier for me than for you."

"D'you think I ought to let you?"

"Why not? It'd probably be better for him to be told by a complete stranger. He'd be compelled to control himself more. Why not let me?"

"It won't be for more than two years. Will we still know each other then?"

"That's up to you. I shall always want to know you. And you're quite happy in the office, aren't you?"

"Oh—very. But it's so unfair to you."

"Nonsense. How can it be unfair if I want it that way? You simply don't know how happy I am just to be with you. There's a limited amount of happiness in the world for most of us. It's wonderful to have found this much. And it's all due to you. Whatever happens, I shall always have you to thank."

"It's the other way round," said Eleanor. "You've meant so much to me. And helped me so much. And, now that you know everything, there's a weight lifted off me that you simply can't imagine. The relief is quite fantastic. I don't know how I've managed up till now. If I'd known what it would have done for me, I'd have told you months ago. Aren't I selfish?"

"It's never selfish to share things—happiness or misery," he said. "I want to give you the one and take away the other."

"You have already helped me so much. It just doesn't seem possible. I shall always be so grateful. It won't be half so difficult now making up all those stories about Hugh. Now I've got you to share it with. Oh, thank you, thank you."

But, while they were talking, Randolph was having the happiest night he had had in prison. Wide-awake, but happy.

15 Good News

THAT MORNING THE GOVERNOR HAD SENT FOR him. The post of prison governor is not one which, on the face of it, appears particularly cheerful. But the governor of Randolph's prison was a particularly cheerful man, firm but sympathetic, and with a gay sense of humor.

"Ah, West," he said, when Randolph had been brought in. "Are you doing anything particular tomorrow?"

Randolph gaped. It wasn't possible. But he liked the governor and he couldn't believe that such a man would indulge in flippancy at a prisoner's expense. It must mean . . . it must mean . . . but he'd had no warning of it . . . he mustn't take things for granted . . . how stupid of him . . . he was going to be asked to get up another theatrical show . . . what a fool to think of anything else. All this in less than a second.

"No, sir," he said, "nothing particular." He hesitated and then: "Just a few odd jobs," he couldn't resist saying.

The governor looked at him sharply for a moment, and then smiled.

"I've good news for you," he said. "Very good news. Almost the best possible, in fact."

Then he was right. Theatrical show! God! This was wonderful. And he'd be seeing Hugh perhaps tomorrow. He felt a lump in his throat and hoped he'd have got rid of it before he had to speak.

The governor mercifully went on speaking.

"Tomorrow," he said, "I shall have the great pleasure of letting you out on parole."

The lump remained. The governor, who had been proposing to wait for Randolph to say something, saw what the position was and went on speaking.

"I'm not a person," he said, "who believes in raising people's hopes for nothing. I think it's a terrible thing to do. Some people don't agree with me. They say that some hope is better than nothing, even if in the end the disappointment is all the greater. They may be right in some cases, but in my view it's very wrong to let a man think that he may be released and then have to tell him later that he isn't going to be. I'll tell you what's happened. For some months now the Home Office has been looking into your conviction. One of the policemen in your case was charged a little time ago with planting evidence. Eventually, he made a full confession in that case—and in yours. He was convinced that you were guilty, his own little boy had once been frightened by a man, and he was determined that you should not get away with it. So he planted the strands on your coat. Ten minutes ago I had it on the telephone. I have no doubt that in due course you will receive a free pardon, but these things must take a few days. I can't let you out till tomorrow, as I've heard nothing officially. But I wouldn't tell you this unless I were quite certain that it will be official. Tomorrow morning I will be authorized to release you on parole. And I hope that within a very short time you will receive a free pardon."

Randolph still could not speak.

"I can't tell you how pleased I am," went on the governor, prepared to go on with his solo for a considerable time, if necessary. "I don't often have this sort of pleasure. I congratulate you. Now, there are one or two things to do and I shall want to know your wishes. You are so far the only person to have been informed. Do you wish anyone else to be told? Do you want to be met at the prison, and, if so, by whom? You're not married, but I am naturally aware of the position. Would you like Miss Parton to be told at once, or what? I dare say you'd like to think things over. It must be a shock. And even a pleasant shock takes it out of a chap. It would me, I can tell you. Now, what about it? Anyone else to be told? Or d'you want to walk in and surprise them?"

Randolph eventually found his voice.

"Thank you, sir, very much," he said. "And thank you for telling me so soon. There can't be any mistake, I suppose?"

"I wouldn't have taken a chance on that," said the governor. "No, I spoke to the Permanent Secretary myself, and he assures me that it's only a question of routine and documents now. Officer, let Mr. West have a chair."

It would have been a shame, the governor had thought, if Randolph had fainted, fallen and broken his neck. And he certainly looked as though he could have done the first. The use of the "Mr." had an electrifying effect on the prison officer. He rushed to a chair and placed it behind Randolph.

"Thank you," said Randolph to the warder. "Thank you, sir," he added to the governor.

"Oh, no," repeated the governor, "I wouldn't have sent for you and told you what I have, if there'd been the least doubt of it. Now, as regards telling other people, I can't do anything about that until I get the written authority. Theoretically there's no confirmation and the press mustn't get hold of it before then. You're another matter. It would have been inhuman not to tell you at once, but I repeat that I wouldn't have dreamed of doing so if there were any chance of my information being wrong."

"Well," said Randolph, forcing himself to think—he found it almost as difficult to face his sudden release as he had found it to face his sentence two years previously—"Well, sir, I think that, as you can't tell anyone tonight, I'll break the good news myself in the morning."

"Very good," said the governor. "But if you change your mind overnight, I'll have a messenger sent as soon as I get my written authority."

So Randolph, indeed, had a happy night. A wonderful night. Anticipation is sometimes better than realization. He could think of a good many happy occasions which had been preceded by even happier anticipation. Indeed, sometimes the fulfillment was almost a bathos. But not in this case. Hugh and Eleanor would be his again. Hugh first, yes, very much first. But Eleanor a good second. She had been so wonderful to him while in prison. He adored her letters, filled with accounts of Hugh's progress. She never missed a letter or a visit, and she seemed to watch for every change in Hugh so that she could tell him about it. He hadn't really been away from the boy at all. How lucky he was to have them both. And soon he would be able to marry her. What a wonderful wife she had been to him in everything but name. And what a wonderful mother. It must have been dreadful for her while he was in prison. But he'd make it up to her now. And they needn't be ashamed of him now. He was to have a free pardon. What a godsend! He had worried a good deal about the effect of his conviction and imprisonment on Hugh. Just as Eleanor had, though in his case with never a thought of giving up the boy because of it. But all that was past. He would not only be free but unconvicted. A man of good character, like everyone else. He'd be able to earn his living in the normal way. No going round looking for jobs, explaining about his conviction. He could hear some of the replies which he would have received:

"Very frank of you to have told me, Mr. West, but I'm afraid we've nothing in your line for the moment. If you'll leave your address we'll write to you if we have anything." Or: "This is a highly confidential post. I assume you can supply the strictest references?" To which he could cheerfully reply:

"I'm sure the governor of the prison where I was will give me an excellent character. I earned full remission marks."

None of that now. People who knew him by sight might look at him now but only as a man who had been wronged, not as a wrongdoer. "How can he have endured it?" they would say to themselves. "How terrible for an innocent man to be in prison for two years." They would look at him with a kind of admiration. He had endured and come through. And without making a fuss. He had done it all with dignity. He had appealed to the Court of Criminal Appeal. Once only. He had petitioned the Home Office once only. There had been no frantic addenda to his petition. He had taken all the legal courses open to him with the help of his legal advisers. He had made no impassioned protestations of innocence, no wild allegations against other people, no pleas to the press to take up his case. He had simply said he was innocent and, when the jury said he was guilty, he had sought to prove that they were wrong. And at last he had won. And he would behave with the same dignity now. The press would, no doubt, want to interview him. He would answer their questions with calm and dignity. Did he want compensation? That was a matter for his legal advisers. Nothing can compensate for imprisonment. He was going on with his life where he had left off. He would do his best to forget the past. Did he want to say anything about the policeman who had given evidence against him? Certainly not. He had never cared to revile people, even if they had done him an injury. And so on. No allegations, no protestations, no pleas. I knew I was innocent. I hoped that I should one day prove it. I am thankful that this has now been done. What was it like in prison? You can best learn by going there, he would say.

And now for tomorrow. He would take them by surprise. He visualized the meeting. It would be a shock, as the governor's statement was to him, but the happiness when Eleanor realized that he had not escaped but was free forever! Hugh, of course, would not know him. He would have seen his photograph, no doubt, but that was not enough for a child of his age. But Eleanor had kept the boy full of the knowledge of his father who would come back to them as soon as he could. He must be careful in his first approach to the boy. He *must* remember that he would probably be a stranger, for all Eleanor's efforts. Very gently, very gradually he would seek the boy's confidence. He must on no account be presumptuous. Children could be as forbidding as dowager duchesses of the old school. He must keep his place. It might take a week, a month or much longer, but he would be patient or the boy might be resentful of this strange man taking liberties with him. But in the end all would be well. His son would know him as he knew his son. Father and son. This is my son. My son. It really was going to happen. Then he actually fell asleep.

16 The Boy in the Garden

THEY CALLED A TAXI FOR HIM AND AT NINE o'clock he was on his way home. Nothing had yet appeared in the newspapers. He felt strange and nervous. No one who has not been imprisoned can appreciate the feelings of a person newly released. The realization that he was going to meet his fellow men on equal terms gave him a curious sensation. On the whole, a happy one, but with an element of fear in it. Rather like when as a small boy he was first selected to play cricket for his school. He remembered the flutters in the pit of his stomach as he walked out to bat. He was batting for the school. They had chosen him out of all those others. He was one of only eleven. He remembered with regret that he was bowled first ball. No longer the exciting flutters in the pit of his stomach. Just deep misery, misery which persisted until he made a glorious catch to win the game. The spectators had risen and cheered him wildly. He had redeemed his duck. What a wonderful tea it was afterward. But for that catch he could not have eaten a thing; he was still numb with misery until that ball came speeding his way not more than a few inches from the ground. Somehow he had flung himself at it and held it. What a moment. And now he was going out to bat again. But he'd be more careful with his wicket this time, much more careful. He would resist the temptation to pick the boy up in his arms. He must resist it at all costs. Gently was the word. Gently.

As the taxi turned into the long road where Eleanor now lived, he looked out at the houses. It was a new neighborhood to him. Possibly he had been in it once or twice but he did not know it. When Eleanor moved there she had explained to him that it seemed better to change their neighbors. She did not want their pity, she said, still less their sneers.

They were bright, clean-looking houses with gardens in the front, some of them full of flowers. Yes, it looked a happy place. He had (as he thought) seen pictures of Hugh in the street. At first there was more street than Hugh but, once Eleanor found that the deception had worked, there was much more Hugh than street. All the same, the place did seem in a way familiar to him from the photographs. Suddenly he banged at the front window of the cab and shouted to the driver: "Stop."

He was very angry with himself for losing control for the moment.

"I'm sorry," he added quietly, "I've just seen my son. So I'll get out here and take my case. So sorry to have given you a shock. But, you see, I haven't seen him for two years."

"O.K., guv," said the driver. "Good luck."

"Thanks," said Randolph.

He took his case, paid and grossly overtipped the driver and was about to leave the taxi when the driver stopped him.

"That's too much, guv," he said. "Thanks all the same." And he handed him back the whole of the tip.

Randolph thought of saying: "I've had a free pardon. I'm not just a released criminal," but decided, on the whole, to leave things as they were.

"That's very good of you," he said. He held out his hand and shook the driver's. "Thanks," he said.

"That's O.K., guv," said the driver. "Cheerio."

And he drove off.

Randolph walked back slowly to the garden where he had seen the boy. Eleanor hadn't written about the friend or friends he must be playing with down the road. "Oh, of course," he said to himself, "how stupid of me. Eleanor's out at work and she must leave Hugh here."

He stopped for a moment. He hoped the boy hadn't heard the shout. He must be more careful. Here he was, determined to be quiet and controlled, and, the first moment he sees his son, he gives a great yell and hammers on the window, almost as though he were out of his mind. This must be a lesson to him. He started to walk very slowly to the garden where the boy was. He reached it and looked over the low fence. The boy was sitting by himself. A teddy bear lay beside him.

"Hullo, young man," said Randolph, in as ordinary a voice as he could manage, but it trembled slightly.

The boy looked up.

"Hullo," he said.

"May I come in?" asked Randolph.

The boy did not answer.

"May I?" repeated Randolph.

Still no answer.

Randolph opened the gate quietly and went slowly into the garden. The boy looked at him curiously but did not appear frightened.

"Well," said Randolph, "who d'you think I am?"

The boy continued to stare.

Randolph waited a full three minutes, looking at the boy, who sat there quietly looking back at him at first. Then he turned over and pulled his bear closer to him.

"Don't bite me, bearie," he said, and hugged it.

Eventually, Randolph decided on action and rang the bell. After a short while the door was opened by a pleasant-looking woman dressed for housework.

"Good morning?" she said questioningly.

"How d'you do?" said Randolph. "It's very good of you to look after Hugh while Eleanor's at work."

"I beg your pardon?" said the woman.

"I'm sure Eleanor's most grateful and so am I. But, now I'm back, I don't suppose it'll be necessary. Not so often, anyway. But it *has* been good of you."

The woman looked at him for a moment or two and then said:

"I'm awfully sorry, but I haven't the faintest idea what you're talking about."

Randolph looked at the boy again. There could be no mistake. There was no doubt whatever. He had the photographs with him. He laughed.

"I expect you're surprised to see me. For the moment I thought I must have made a mistake. But that's Hugh all right."

"Who *are* you?" asked the woman.

"How stupid of me," said Randolph. "Of course, you wouldn't know. I'm Hugh's father. Do forgive me for being so stupid."

This is what happens to a man when he comes out of prison, he told himself. He's not used to meeting ordinary people in an ordinary way. I must be frightfully awkward. Just imagine walking into a strange woman's house and not saying at once who he was.

"Yes, I'm the guilty party," he added, trying to find confidence in facetiousness. "D'you think Hugh's like me?"

"Who on earth is Hugh?" asked the woman.

For a moment Randolph wondered whether the boy had wandered into a strange garden. But the woman could see the boy and did not seem in the least surprised at his presence. But perhaps she thought they'd come in together. That must be it. What an ass he was. Of course, that was it.

"Stupid of me," he said. "I do apologize. I thought you must have looked after Hugh while Eleanor's at work. He oughtn't to wander about like this. It's dangerous."

He must really speak to Eleanor about it. Was Hugh really allowed to wander about the street? It must be the people who looked after him. Eleanor couldn't possibly know. Well, he'd soon put a stop to that.

"I suppose you don't happen to know who's supposed to be looking after him while Eleanor's at work?" he asked.

"Looking after whom?"

"Hugh, of course."

"Who is Hugh?"

"Let me introduce you. I'm afraid I don't know your name . . ."

"Watson."

"Hugh, this is Mrs. Watson. Mrs. Watson, this is Hugh."

His first introduction of his son. He'd done it the wrong way round!

"I'm sorry," he went on. "Mrs. Watson, this is Hugh. Hugh, this is Mrs. Watson."

Mrs. Watson imagined she must be dealing with a tame lunatic; at least, she hoped he was tame. Better to humor him, anyway.

"And, if he's Hugh, who are you, may I ask?"

"I'm Hugh's father. I've only just come back."

"May I ask where from?"

"Well," said Randolph, "that doesn't matter. The point is, I'm back."

Escaped from an asylum obviously, thought Mrs. Watson. I must get onto the police. Make an excuse for going inside.

"Forgive me," she said. "I want to speak to my husband before he goes off to work."

Her husband had left the house some time before, but she felt it was as well to let the stranger think that there was a man in the house.

"Of course," said Randolph. "I'll talk to Hugh."

A sudden fear took hold of the woman. Lunatics, however quiet they seemed, might suddenly do anything. Kidnap the boy or even kill him. She'd take no chances.

"Come along, Georgie," she said to the child. "Come in with Mummy."

"Want to play with bearie," said the boy.

"You can play with bearie inside," said Mrs. Watson. "Come along, now. Don't keep Mummy waiting."

Reluctantly the boy got up, still holding his bear, and walked into the house. Mrs. Watson shut the door.

Randolph waited, puzzled. What an odd woman. And Hugh hadn't been wandering around. This was obviously the place where Eleanor left him. And the woman called him Georgie. Well, there wasn't much in that. People sometimes called children by different names. But to shut the door on him seemed rather odd. And asking all those questions. But, of course, he thought, I'm not married to Eleanor. She can't have the faintest idea who I am. I might be a kidnapper or a lunatic or something. How could she tell I was Hugh's father? Stupid of me. I should have produced the photographs. He could soon put that right. He rang the bell. Nothing happened. He rang again. Still no result. He listened and could hear talking going on, but not what was said. It's all very odd, he thought. But, anyway, I'm back, and Hugh is only a few yards away. Probably it was silly of me to try to surprise them. Ridiculous. Of course Eleanor will be at work. But not for much longer, now that he was back. No more finding places for Hugh to be while she was out. A mother ought to be with her child, if possible. Dr. Spock said that a child needs individual care up to the age of three. Much better that that care should come from the mother. Well, it would in future. The important period was from one to three, but he felt sure that Eleanor had done the best that could be done in the circumstances. Her letters showed that. He rang the bell again. There was still no answer. It was all very odd. A few minutes later a police car arrived. Two policemen got out and came into the garden.

"Good morning, sir," one of them said.

"Good morning," said Randolph, and was surprised at his lack of fear. A policeman was now his friend, no longer his jailer.

"D'you live here, sir?" asked the officer.

"No," said Randolph.

"Then may I ask your business here?"

"Certainly," said Randolph. "I've called for my son."

"Your son?"

"Yes."

"We've just been telephoned by the lady of the house to say that it's *her* son."

"Her son!" said Randolph incredulously. "I suppose she's playing some sort of game. But personally I'm getting a bit tired of it. Look, officer . . ."

Randolph got out his pocketbook and took out some of the photographs. "Look at these," he said.

Both officers looked at the photographs.

"They don't tell us much without seeing the boy," the first officer said.

"Have a look at him," said Randolph. "He's inside."

The officers looked at each other and then one of them rang the bell. Before the door was opened, Mrs. Watson looked out of a window to see who it was. Seeing the police, she went to the door and opened it at once. The boy was with her. The officer looked at the photographs and then at the boy. There was no doubt about it. They were the same. Neither of them said anything for the moment. They just looked at the photographs, then at the boy, and then at the photographs again.

"It's him, all right," said one to the other.

This is a rum do, all right, they said to themselves. We're called here about a lunatic, but which is it? Eventually, one of them spoke.

"Mrs. Watson?" he asked.

"That's me," said Mrs. Watson.

"Do you say the child is your son, Madam?"

"Of course I do. Why on earth d'you have to ask me?"

"Well, this gentleman has a lot of photographs of him and *he* says it's *his* son."

"Nonsense," said Mrs. Watson. "Let me see."

They handed her the photographs. She looked at them and was surprised at first. Then she relaxed.

"Of course," she said. "I can explain now. Though I don't know who this gentleman is. There's a Mrs. West up the road who asked if she might take photographs of Georgie. I didn't mind. So she's been taking them ever since."

Randolph went white, but managed to speak.

"I am Randolph West," he said.

And then with horror he realized what must have happened. Hugh had died and Eleanor daren't tell him while he was in prison. So she had pretended that he was alive and taken the photographs of another child of the same age. Yes, he remembered now. It all fitted in. He had complained that the first photographs really showed nothing of the child, and then that they were badly taken. The wrong light, the camera must have moved, overdeveloped, underdeveloped, and so on. It was only later that good photographs started to appear. Oh, God! Hugh was dead. His son dead. But poor Eleanor. How she must have suffered. How terrible for her to have to bear this burden alone. Well, she would have him to help her now. But who was to help *him?* His son. The one thought that had made his time in prison possible. And he was dead!

The policeman saw how Randolph had changed and put out a hand to steady him.

"Are you all right, sir?" he asked.

"Yes," said Randolph drearily, "I'm all right. I'm sorry to have caused all this trouble. I've been away, and my son—my son is dead."

He walked through the gate and along the street. Mrs. Watson and the police officers stayed chatting together.

One word ran through Randolph's mind as he walked. Dead. Dead. For some time his mind was so numb with the shock that it could do nothing else but reiterate "dead." But after a time some feeling returned and he tried to think when Hugh must have died. He soon realized that it must have been very early in his imprisonment. When he had the first bad photographs. But what did it matter *when* he died? He was dead. Where was he buried? He visualized the pathetic tiny grave. What had Eleanor put on it? What did it matter? Hugh was dead. The little person whom he had left with his smiling mouth and bright eyes, his chuckles and his tears, was dead. Why? What was the cause of death? Could it have been prevented? What did that matter? It had not been prevented. Hugh was dead. The gradual coming together of father and son which he had so often visualized in his cell would never happen, never, at any rate, until he was dead too. He could not even wish that he were. His mind was incapable of wishing. Incapable of anything. It was as dead as a living mind in a sane and living person can be.

17 The Lawyers Prepare

ELEANOR WAS IN JEREMY NORTON'S ROOM AT THE
office when she heard of Randolph's release. Jeremy had turned
on the news, and she listened to the announcement with a mixture of fear and pleasure.

"What can I do?" she asked. "He'll probably be at home by
now, waiting for me. I'm surprised he hasn't rung me here to
know where Hugh is."

"I'll come along with you, if you like," replied Jeremy.

"No, I'll have to do it myself now," she said. "There's no
alternative. But I can't think what will happen. D'you think I
could possibly leave now? I must get it over. Until it is, I
couldn't do anything properly here."

"Of course," said Jeremy. "Go off straightway. And take
tomorrow off too, if you want it. If you get a chance, perhaps
you'd phone me to tell me what happened. I do want to know.
And, in any event, if you want any kind of help, you've only to
say."

"You are kind," she said.

Within five minutes she was on her way home, wondering how she could break the news. She knew what his first question would be: "Where's Hugh?" She would have to parry it and kiss him and say she wanted to talk to him. He'd realize from her tone of voice that something was wrong and that might help to break the shock. Poor Randolph. She felt infinite pity for him. Would he hate her for it? He must. She had put out of his reach the one thing on earth which he had lived for. From his point of view it must seem a merciless crime. She took a taxi home. He was in the sitting room, heard the taxi door bang, and guessed that it was Eleanor. He had been sitting in an armchair, staring blankly at the carpet. But he must make an effort for Eleanor's sake. He was standing by the door when she arrived. She could see from the look in his face that something was terribly wrong. But he couldn't know yet.

He took her in his arms and kissed her. Then he held her away from him and looked at her.

"It's good to be back," he said, "but—oh, my darling . . ." and he broke off.

"D'you know?" she asked incredulously.

He nodded, then took her in his arms again.

"Oh, God!" he said. "Why did it have to be?"

"How did you find out?" she asked.

"Mrs. Watson told me."

"Mrs. Watson! She doesn't know."

"I mean, I realized from what she told me."

"I see."

But how, thought Eleanor, could he have guessed from anything that Mrs. Watson had said.

"Darling," he said, "I don't want to make things worse for you—but I must know where he is—where he is buried."

"Buried?" said Eleanor. "Who d'you mean?"

"Hugh, of course. Why do you ask?"

"Come and sit down," said Eleanor, and led him to a couch where they sat together for some time in silence.

"Darling," said Eleanor, "I want you to prepare for a shock."

"There is nothing left to shock me."

"There is," said Eleanor. "Hugh is not dead."

He jumped to his feet.

"Not dead?" he said excitedly, but, seeing Eleanor's face, he realized that it was not good news which she had to tell.

"In a home? A hospital? Crippled? Can he recognize you? I must see him, whatever state he's in. Is it the mind or the body, or both? Tell me, tell me. I must know."

"As far as I know, darling, Hugh is alive and happy and well."

"Then where is he? What are you saying? I don't understand. Everyone seems mad today. Mrs. Watson down the road, and now you. What are you telling me?"

"He's been adopted."

"Adopted? But they can't do that. Just because I was sent to prison, they can't take the child away. You were able to look after Hugh. What are you telling me? You couldn't have consented?"

"I did consent, my darling."

"You consented? You couldn't have. It's impossible. You loved him as I did. You wrote to me about him. Oh—God! Those photographs. Your letters. All lies. But why, my darling, why? I don't understand. Where is he, and why did you do it?"

She explained as best she could. He understood better than she had expected. From time to time he could not help saying:

"Oh, darling, why did you do it? Why did you?" And then he began to ask questions about the adopters, which Eleanor could not answer. All at once he said:

"But could they do this without my consent?"

"They told me at the adoption society that, as we weren't married, your consent wasn't necessary."

"But I'd lived with the child for a year. Surely that makes a difference?"

"I didn't tell them that, I'm afraid," said Eleanor. "I was so anxious to get it over with the least possible fuss that I said I'd only met you once at a dance and didn't know who you were, except that you were a solicitor."

"And they just accepted all you said?"

"They'd no reason to disbelieve me. That's why I moved, of course, to be out of the neighborhood where we'd lived. In case the truth might have come out."

"I'm going to take legal advice," said Randolph. "I'm not giving up without a struggle."

"But would it be good for Hugh to come back to us after two years?"

"He's ours. I want him. I need him desperately. You can't think what I've been through, waiting and waiting in prison. It was Hugh who kept me going. If it's humanly possible, I must get him back. I believe I'd almost *take* him back."

"You'd only lose him again, and probably go to prison. For something you *had* done this time. And think of Hugh being bashed about like a tennis ball."

"Yes, I see that," said Randolph. "No, I wouldn't really take him. But I'm going to see if we can get him back legally. I'm sure he'd settle down with us again after a month or two. After all, he was with us for his first twelve months. That must make a difference."

"Why not come and see Jeremy Norton? He's been wonderfully kind to me, and I know he'd do anything to help."

"Who's he?"

Eleanor blushed slightly.

"He's a partner in the solicitors I work for."

She paused for a moment.

"And he's been so kind to me."

"A boy friend?" he asked.

"Sort of," she said.

"Why not?" he replied. "You couldn't be expected to go into a nunnery while I was away."

She kissed him.

"You do understand," she said. "Let's go and see him."

So next morning they kept an appointment with Jeremy in his office. The first thing he wanted to see were the papers that had been served on Eleanor. She had kept them and brought them with her to the interview. He looked at them and then he said:

"That's odd."

"What's odd?" asked Randolph.

"Oh—nothing," said Jeremy. "Just a technical matter. Now, tell me," he went on, "all three of you lived together for just about a year?"

"Yes."

"And who paid the household expenses?"

"I did," said Randolph, "naturally."

"So, in effect, you were living like husband and wife, the husband keeping the family?"

"Exactly."

"The only difference being that you weren't actually married?"

"Yes."

"Well," said Jeremy after a little thought, "it seems to me that it can be argued that there was an agreement by you to maintain the child. Such an agreement doesn't have to be in writing. Agreements can be made by conduct. They are, every day. For example, if you go into a shop and pick up an article and hand the assistant the price without either of you saying a word, there's an agreement by the one of you to buy and the other to sell the article. If you park your car on a piece of private land which has 'Parking 2/6 an hour' on it, you agree to pay 2/6 for every hour by leaving your car there. In the same way, by keeping the child week after week, it can be said that there was what lawyers would call an implied agreement by you to keep the child, if only temporarily. All the law requires is that there should be an agreement by you to maintain the child. It doesn't even say for how long. One of you hasn't to say solemnly to the other, 'Do you agree to maintain this child?' and the other answer 'Yes,' to make an agreement. If you both intended that Mr. West should maintain the child indefinitely and he actually did so for a year, in my view there's ample material for the Court to say that there was an agreement under which you were liable to support the child."

"Where does all this lead to?" asked Randolph.

"Well, if I'm right about that, and I can't guarantee that I am—I think we should get counsel's opinion on the matter—but if he confirms my view, it seems that Mr. West was entitled to be served with the proceedings and to be heard by the Court before an order was made."

"But how could they serve him," asked Eleanor, "if they didn't know of his existence?"

"Well, at least they could have tried a bit harder to find out. But whether they could or could not have found him, the fact remains that you weren't served and, if I'm right about the agreement part of it, you were entitled to be served."

"Was my consent necessary then?"

"No, it wasn't."

"Then what difference would my being served have made?"

"You would have been entitled to go before the judge and object to an order being made. He could, of course, have refused to give effect to your objection. In many cases—in most cases—a putative father wouldn't have any chance of stopping an adoption. But a case like yours is different. You might have been living together for ten years, for example. In such a case, unquestionably, a judge might take a good deal of notice of what a putative father had to say. And there's a further strong point in your favor. You intended to marry Miss Parton, if and when you got a divorce."

"I still do."

"Fine. Well, if you marry, that will make Hugh legitimate. Now, supposing you'd gone before the judge and told him all that two years ago, he might—I don't say he would—but he might have refused an adoption order. Of course, a good deal would have depended on what arrangements could have been made to look after the child. A child of one needs a mother very badly. You'd have been asked what you could do about that. If Miss Parton had assented to the adoption, and didn't change her mind, it might have been very difficult, if not impossible, for you to satisfy the judge that an order shouldn't be made, but you had the right to argue about it. But then, I suppose, it's possible that, if Miss Parton had known—and, of course, she would have known—that you were going to the Court to object, she might have withdrawn her consent."

"I certainly would have," said Eleanor.

"Well, if you had, I don't see how a judge could have made the order. So, if Mr. West had been served, the probability is that an order would never have been made. But, even if it could have been made, Mr. West lost the chance of being heard on the matter. And, in my view, if he was liable to support the child under an agreement, I believe he has a right to have the order set aside. That doesn't necessarily mean that you'll get Hugh back."

"Then what's the point of it all?" asked Randolph.

"It means that you'd have a reasonable chance of getting him back. And that would be something, wouldn't it?"

"It would, indeed," said Randolph. "But what would it depend on?"

"A good many things," said Jeremy. "But, first of all, let's find out if my view about an agreement is right. And there's another thing we want to get on with. That's your divorce."

"It can't be too soon for me."

"Good. Then, if you agree, I'll fix up a conference with counsel and go into the whole matter."

Eleanor and Randolph left in a much happier frame of mind than when they arrived at Jeremy's office.

In the meantime, Hugh was paddling happily in a pool in the Woodthorpes' garden, while Mary and Bill were watching him equally happily. They had not yet heard the announcement of Randolph's release. Hugh had now been with them two years and was a cheerful and promising three-year-old.

It was not until the evening that Bill heard about Randolph's release. Eric had given his name only as West, and there might have been more than one West in prison, but he felt sure it was Hugh's father. So he had to tell Mary. She was horrified and he tried to calm her.

"We can't be certain it's the same man," he said.

"But you think it is."

"I can't help thinking it is, but it may not be."

"When will we know?"

"It's impossible to say. And, anyway, we don't know that, if he's the man, he'll try to do anything about it. But I promise you this. If any attempt is made to take Hugh from us, we'll go abroad at once and I'll sell up everything."

"You are good to me," she said.

"But I'd hate to lose Hugh."

"So you would, darling. You'd hate to lose him. But I'd die without him. I love you, darling, but I can't live without Hugh. I mean, I couldn't live if someone took him away from us. It would be different if he died. I'd be heartbroken but it couldn't be avoided. But I couldn't live knowing he was alive somewhere else and couldn't be with us."

"Well, you won't have to," said Bill. "Very likely we'll hear nothing more about it. But, if we do, then we'll be off and away."

"Thank God for you," said Mary.

On the way home from Jeremy's office, Eleanor very tentatively mentioned a subject which had been troubling her. She was devoted to Randolph and wanted to try to make up to him for the two terrible years in prison but, at the back of her mind, she was intensely worried about Hugh. He had now had two years with another family. What effect would a change at the age of three have on him? She had read and listened to comprehensible and less comprehensible pronouncements by psychiatrists on the effect of lack of security on a child. Might not another change damage the child? How she wished that she had not yielded to her overwhelming feeling that she must give Hugh away when Randolph was sent to prison. She was not in the least conscience-stricken. She still felt that what she had done was right. Of course, if she had known what was going to happen, she wouldn't have dreamed of doing it. But how could she know? The jury had found him guilty, the judge had sentenced him, the Appeal Court had dismissed his appeal, and the Home Secretary had refused to interfere. Randolph had still assured her of his innocence, but how could such an assurance prevail against all the forces of the law? And, even if she had fully believed in him, the fact would have remained that he would have served seven years in prison and been known for the rest of his life as a criminal or ex-criminal, and a sex maniac as well.

But, although she did not reproach herself, she expected Randolph to reproach her. It was only natural. From his point of view she must have let him down horribly. What a terrible thing to do to a man, and then to follow it up by the other lies. But Randolph was incredibly understanding and, although at first he did say twice, "Oh, Eleanor, how could you?" he soon ceased to reproach her at all. He concentrated entirely on getting Hugh back.

"Darling," said Eleanor, "you are sure that it'll be all right for Hugh for us to get him back?"

"All right?" he said. "We're his parents. We made him. He has our bodies and minds in him and no one else's. Of course, he'll be a bit unhappy at first, and feel strange with us. But we had him for a year. That's only two years ago. He'll soon be ours in every sense."

"It'll be rather awful for the other people."

"I know," said Randolph. "It was more than rather awful for me in prison, but I had to stand it. And, after all, they can get another. This isn't their child. They chose it like you might choose an animal. Oh—I know it isn't the same thing after you've got it, but, in the first instance, they couldn't have any love for a child whom they'd never seen before. And they ought to have tried to find me before they took it."

"That was my fault," said Eleanor. "I lied about you. So how could they tell?"

"I see that," said Randolph. "And it will be hard on them. But it would be harder still on me. I've been robbed of two years of my life. It can't be right that I should be robbed of my son as well."

She saw that it would be hopeless to pursue the matter and

did not try again. She also felt that, after what she had done, she was hardly the right person to seek to persuade Randolph from trying to get back the child.

The next morning Jeremy sent for her.

"I've been thinking about this case," he said to her. "Now, are you quite sure that you want me to try to get the boy back?"

"Absolutely," said Eleanor.

"Right," said Jeremy. "If you want him back, I'll get him back. You know there's nothing that I wouldn't do for you."

"You are much too good," she said.

"Pure self-interest," he said. "I'd prefer to be happy myself, but the next best thing is to see you happy. Now, there's one thing we ought to do at once, just in case of accidents."

"What's that?"

"Make the boy a ward of court."

"What for?"

"It's only a precautionary measure, but it's just worth taking."

"But why, and what is it?"

"Well, I know it's most unlikely, but supposing, when we've issued an application to have the adoption order set aside, the other people took fright and went abroad? I know it's rather farfetched, but such things do happen. Once they were abroad, there'd be nothing you could do about it. If we make the child a ward of court, he can't go abroad without the High Court's permission, and that would never be given until our application had been disposed of. So I'll get Mr. West's authority and do it straightway."

"But can a child be made a ward of court just like that?"

"Pretty well. All you have to do is to settle some money on the infant, it doesn't matter how little, and apply for it to be made a ward of court. From the moment you apply, the child is a ward of court. It's too simple, really. But that's the law, and I'd better get on with it—just in case."

It was a dreadful day for Mary when she was given the terrible news. The first definite notice which she and Bill had that Randolph West was the child's father, and was going to do something about it, was when they received notice that an application was being made to make him a ward of court. At first she wanted to go abroad just the same. But it was pointed out to her that, once the application was made, the child could not be taken abroad without the Court's permission, so that the result might be that, if they tried to get out of the country without permission and failed, both she and Bill might go to prison and would certainly have prejudiced their chances of keeping Hugh.

"It's so cruel," said Mary. "They can't take Hugh away from us now."

"I don't suppose they will," said Bill, "but they've got to hear both sides first. Anyway, you remember that Luttrell said that no judge in his senses would decide against us. I know it's dreadful to have it hanging over us, darling, but you must try not to worry too much. It'll be all right in the end. Just as it was when that fellow blackmailed you. And, if you look too worried, Hugh will notice and then he'll be upset."

Once having made Hugh a ward of court, Jeremy issued an application in the Court of Appeal, asking for the order to be set aside on the ground that Randolph had never been served with the proceedings and that, as he was a person who had agreed to maintain the child, he was entitled to have been served. Counsel had advised that this was the right course to take.

Judge Bramcote was told about the application.

"But this is very odd," he said. "How does the father know the name of the adopters? He could still have made his application, even if he hadn't, but it's very odd that he knows it."

This was a fact which had puzzled every lawyer who had had

to deal with the case. All prospective adopters have the right to ask that their cases shall be heard under a serial number, so that their names and addresses shall not be made known to the mother or father of the child. As Judge Bramcote said, this would not prevent the parents from making an application in the case because they would know the number of the case and the Court in which it was brought. At any time they could make any proper application and the Court, although it would not disclose the name of the adopters, would serve notice of the application upon them. Nor would the fact that the parents did not know the names of the adopters prevent them from making the child a ward of court, as the child could be identified. In Hugh's case, he would have been described as the infant formerly known as Hugh Parton, the son of Eleanor Parton, born on such and such a day, in respect of whom an adoption order was made on such and such a day in such and such a Court. Unless the adopters had gone abroad, there would be no difficulty in serving them with the application. So the use of a serial number is no protection whatever against the possibility of an application to set aside an adoption order by a father who has not been served with the application for adoption when he had a right to be served with it.

But, all the same, it seemed very odd to Judge Bramcote that Randolph's solicitor knew the adopters' name and address. This was, in fact, due to one of those mistakes that are occasionally made even by the most careful people. A clerk in the County Court had, by mistake, sent a copy of the adoption order to Eleanor. This contained the name and address of Mary and Bill and it ought never to have been sent to her. It was this that had enabled Eric to start blackmailing Mary. There were other ways in which he might have found out, but they would probably have entailed making a lot of inquiries, and the probability is that he would have been unable to do so. Strangers would be more likely to learn of an adoption if they lived in the adopters' neighborhood. And, if anyone in the neighborhood happened to have a mind like Eric's, he might have found out enough to act as he did. But the refined torture of blackmail is most unlikely when a serial number has been used, although it is not impossible. And, of course, mistakes are occasionally made. In any event, an application to set aside an adoption order by a putative father who has been ignored and has a right to be heard is in no way avoided by the use of a serial number.

When Judge Bramcote heard about the mistake, he was very angry but, beyond ensuring that the error of their ways was pointed out to all those who were responsible, there was nothing he could do about it. And, indeed, being quite unaware of Eric's previous activities, he imagined that no harm, in fact, had been done.

"But it might have been," he said. "The mother might have tried to kidnap the child, if she had changed her mind too late. Too much care cannot be taken over these matters."

The judge said this to the registrar, who was responsible for the conduct of the proceedings of the Court. The registrar said his little piece to the chief clerk. The chief clerk spoke strongly to the staff clerk in charge of adoptions, and the staff clerk took it out on a senior clerk, who was very angry with the junior clerk who had caused all the trouble. But the fact remained that it had happened.

Both sides now prepared for battle, but it was agreed between the solicitors that it would probably be better to start the proceedings in the County Court rather than go straight to the Court of Appeal. They considered that this course might save time and expense. Judge Bramcote decided that it would be better if Judge Hazlewell heard the application.

Mr. Luttrell advised Bill and Mary to employ a woman barrister.

"You think she'll understand a case like this better than a man?" said Bill.

"Partly that, but mainly because she's a very able person and as tenacious as a bulldog. Once she's got her teeth into anything, she just won't let go."

So a few days later Mary and Bill and Mr. Luttrell attended Mrs. Boulder's chambers in the Temple.

"Sit you down," she said, after being introduced, and then she looked at Mary.

"Mrs. Woodthorpe," she said, "I recognize that these proceedings are and will be a tremendous strain for you. I've had children of my own and know all about it. But you must try to control yourself. If you're going to weep in my chambers— which at the moment seems highly probable—what'll you do before the judge? Now, some people might think that was an advantage. Well, it isn't. At some stage in the case the judge may ask himself whether he is to send back the child to the home of a tearful woman, who can't control herself."

"I haven't cried in your chambers, and I'm not going to," said Mary rather crossly.

"That's because I'm being beastly to you," said Mrs. Boulder. "The judge may be, and probably will be, exactly the opposite. He may even weep himself. Just think what the poor fellow's got to do. On the one side, he has two admirable people who want the boy. On the other side, he has two equally admirable people who want him just as much. One side is going to be brokenhearted. If the judge had, by law, to strike you in the face, he'd refuse to do it. He'd resign his office and let someone else do the dirty work. But he's got to do much worse than that. He's got to tear the heart out of one of you. I don't know how he can do it. If he lets you keep the child, that man who has served two years in prison will find himself robbed of his child without any fault on his part, except perhaps that he shouldn't have had it in the first instance. If the judge gives him back the child, you'll be quite desperate. Poor fellow, I say. I shouldn't like to bear his burden. I'll never be a judge for that reason. I suppose there have been judges who appeared to have been able to drink their port all right after sentencing someone to death. There had to be, in the old days, when death was the penalty for petty stealing. But I wouldn't have that job for the world. So, when you're feeling sorry for yourself, spare a thought for the poor old judge."

Mary and Bill could not avoid exchanging glances.

"That's all right," said Mrs. Boulder. "I wanted to stop you feeling too sorry for yourselves before we began. Now, let's get down to business. Hugh, I gather from your statement, is the perfect boy. That, if I may say so, is a pity. A perfect boy, if suddenly removed from you to a strange environment, is less likely to suffer serious harm. A difficult, highly strung, tearful young man would be much better from our point of view. Now, I'm not suggesting for one moment that you should make up a case about him. Of course not. For one thing, we don't do that sort of thing and, for another, the judge will probably see the boy and, if he's a normal, cheerful boy, he's not going to burst into tears and bite the judge's little finger. But every child has faults and I want you to think about them very carefully. From the bad habits like biting nails to the worst things like sulking. I want you to try to think of him quite objectively and to make a list of all his defects, physical, mental and moral. He's old enough at three to have some of each. My children, I suppose, were like most fond mothers' children—the best in the world —but I could have recited a list of their faults. Mark you, I shouldn't have dreamed of doing so. They were quite perfect, I assure you."

"But what good will this do?" asked Bill.

"It'll please me, for one thing," said Mrs. Boulder, "and the reason it'll please me is because, when you've done it, Mr. Luttrell will take the list to a psychiatrist, preferably one who has not himself been certified. It doesn't need a psychiatrist to tell you that to remove Hugh from you now must be bad for the boy. But how bad? That's the question. And we want a man who'll make it as bad as bad can be. We want a man who thinks he really understands children and may be right. We want a man who is convinced that most neuroses can be traced back to childhood. It would be very nice if we could get a man who would be prepared to say that, if this child were taken from you now, he might conceivably go to the bad when he grows up."

"Have you any suggestions, Mrs. Boulder?" asked Mr. Luttrell.

"Let me see," said Mrs. Boulder. "This judge doesn't like psychiatrists, but he's got to have them in this case. Now, let's see. Who is there? What about Crestway? Bit of a paranoiac, but, unless you get him on his pet aversion, he's really quite sane. And lucid. He always speaks to you as though you were a dull pupil in the lowest form at school. That's the way I like to be spoken to when I don't understand the subject. He's excellent for most judges, though his didactic methods do rile some of them. The only danger with him would be if someone happened to hit on the subject of racing. He must have lost a fiver on a horse once, or something. But he may be talking to you quite sanely and normally and, as I said, most lucidly, if the conversation is about psychiatry, and then, somehow or other, horse racing is mentioned. His whole manner changes. He snorts, rather like a horse, as a matter of fact. And his eyes certainly look at you rather like a horse which has seen a rather alarming piece of paper in the road. And then he begins. He grips you by the arm and a torrent of words comes out of his mouth so fast that he isn't always able to arrange the order properly.

If that was his normal behavior, he'd be certified in a trice. But, fortunately, it isn't. I think he'd be good with Hazlewell. He's a judge who wants to learn. He wants to know why. Crestway will tell him. That's if he's prepared to support us. And I imagine that almost any psychiatrist would be prepared to support us."

"Won't any of them come on behalf of the Wests?"

"Oh, indeed, yes. I said that almost any would come for us. But quite a number would back up the other side. Now, I don't see why anyone should mention racing in this case. I hope not, anyway."

Mrs. Boulder held out her arm.

"I sometimes think I can still feel the bruise he made on my arm when he gripped it."

She thought for a moment.

"I think perhaps we'll keep him in reserve. We may want two. So we'll make Crestway a reserve. Now, who else is there? Ah—I know. Baldry. Frank Baldry. The great thing about him is that no one would ever know he was a psychiatrist. It's his stock in trade. He's aware of the prejudice against his profession and the jokes that are made about it. And it's plain to see that he's studied the art of being ordinary. He'd be a wonderful actor. His throw-away lines are worth listening to."

"'Throw-away lines?'" queried Mary.

"Yes. You know the way an actor will sometimes say something that you can hardly hear. It's either a good joke or very important. The trouble with many actors is that they throw it away so successfully that no one can hear it. But, when they ensure that it is heard, it's a most effective method of advocacy. The sort of thing I mean is this. Suppose Baldry is being examined about a man's mind. He'll describe his findings in a very matter-of-fact tone and end up quite casually with something like: 'The sort of mind, you know, you find in a murderer.' But he throws away 'murderer' so cleverly that, though you hear it perfectly, it sounds as though it only just reached you. It seems so casual, as it does with a good actor, but it's all most carefully studied. Yes, I think Baldry for our number one. Crestway for our reserve. Now, we'd better have someone else in case of accidents. I know. Mallet. He's just the opposite of Baldry. Mallet looks and talks like a psychiatrist. He's a very little man. Rather like a bird, really. What sort of bird? A chicken, I suppose, is the nearest. He'll talk quite slowly for a time and then suddenly he'll see a tempting morsel, something he really feels he knows all about, and peck, peck, peck he goes, peck, peck, peck. He's got all the degrees and he's written a book on dreams and insomnia. Should be in every hotel room, like the Gideon Bibles. He's even invented a method of preselecting your dream. It's a bit complicated and I've never found it to work. But it sent me to sleep all right."

"I'm most grateful for all this advice," said Mary, "but what I want to know is whether we're going to win our case?"

"Fair enough," said Mrs. Boulder. "My opinion is that you will." And then, noticing Mary's immediate pleasure, added: "I can't guarantee that the judge will say the same and, of course, if new facts of which I know nothing emerge, obviously I can't say what the effect will be. Now, if there's nothing else, please prepare that list as quickly as you can, give it to Mr. Luttrell and he'll get on to Baldry, Mallet and Crestway. Try to get some sleep, Mrs. Woodthorpe. The hearing isn't for three weeks and you'll be in no condition to give evidence if you don't. You don't want to arrive pale and bleary-eyed. Leave that to the judge."

Much the same sort of thing was happening to Randolph and Eleanor. Jeremy had also suggested that they should brief a woman, Miss Frayling. She was a most attractive young

woman of thirty-eight, married, with three children. She re-
tained her maiden name for professional purposes. She had a
particularly persuasive smile. Men witnesses sometimes found it
dangerously seductive.

"Well, would you agree with me about this, Mr. Plainfield?"
she would say, with a smile which seemed large enough for the
whole court to bask in, though it was directed solely at Mr.
Plainfield. And Mr. Plainfield had the greatest possible difficulty
in disagreeing. Indeed, it had been said of her that she had
persuaded an independent witness of an accident to say that a
car, which he had sworn was going forward at about twenty
miles an hour, was, in fact, going backward.

She also advised that a psychiatrist should be called for the
purpose of saying that Hugh would come to no harm if he
went back to his real parents. She was particularly anxious
that the divorce proceedings should be speeded up. She pointed
out that, if it could be shown that an undefended divorce petition was on its way to a hearing, it would be a tremendous advantage. On Randolph's and Eleanor's marrying, Hugh would
automatically become legitimate. But an application to postpone
the hearing to enable the divorce to go through and Randolph
and Eleanor to marry was refused by Judge Hazlewell.

"It would be very wrong," he said, in refusing it, "to allow
this matter to be postponed for any time at all unless it is es-
sential. If the boy is to be moved back to his natural parents,
the sooner the better. If he is not to be moved, the parties on
both sides should not be subjected to any further suspense. It
is quite true that, if the applicant were married to the mother
by the time his application is heard, he would have a stronger
case. But if he and Miss Parton say that they intend to marry
as soon as divorce proceedings have made their marriage possible, and if they are believed when they say this, their case
will be nearly as strong as if they were actually married. Not

quite as strong, it is true, but very nearly. And it is to be noted that they have made this application to adjourn the matter. It is opposed—quite properly, I think—by the adoptive parents but, having opposed it, their learned counsel will find it very difficult to ask me not to believe that the natural parents intend to marry. The applicant offered him the proof of the pudding by asking for an adjournment. Having refused this offer, it will be almost impossible for him to satisfy me that it was not a genuine one."

18 *Evidence and Argument*

IN DUE COURSE THE CASE WAS HEARD IN JUDGE Hazlewell's private room. No one wore robes. The judge was in a lounge suit and sat at a table. Mrs. Boulder and Miss Frayling sat opposite him. Their solicitors sat just behind them. Mary and Bill sat behind their solicitors and Randolph and Eleanor behind theirs. At the side of the table, near to the judge, was another chair for the witnesses, and next to the witnesses' chair was a chair for the clerk. It was all rather crowded. Had not the wrong form been sent to Eleanor, the parties would have been kept separate from each other. But, as they each knew each other's names and addresses, there was no point in this.

When everyone was ready, Miss Frayling opened the proceedings. After a few preliminary remarks saying who represented whom, she went on:

"Your Honor, this application (which by consent is made in the first instance to Your Honor instead of the Court of Ap-

peal) is to set aside the adoption order on the simple ground
that my client, Mr. Randolph West, had a right to be heard
before the order was made and that, as he was deprived of that
right, he has an absolute right to have that order set aside."

"Isn't it a matter of discretion?" asked the judge.

"With respect, no, Your Honor," said Miss Frayling. "It is
an elementary principle of English justice that every person who
has a right to be heard on any particular matter shall be given
the opportunity of being heard. That was not done in this case.
Indeed, I may add nobody bothered very much about my client.
They just accepted the mother's say-so that he was not to be
found. If the mother had been brought to court and examined
on oath, she would have had to admit that she knew exactly
where the father was, that she had lived with him as a wife,
and that it was not just a casual affair after a dance."

"Be that as it may," said the judge, "if I set aside the order, I
could still make it again after having heard the father."

"That is so, Your Honor, but . . ."

"It must be very rare for an adoption order to be refused
when the mother consents, just because the putative father ob-
jects."

"I agree, Your Honor," said Miss Frayling.

"Well then," said the judge, "if I hear the putative father's
objections, and consider that they would not have weighed with
me so as to prevent an order being made in the first place,
what is the point of setting aside the order?"

"I will tell Your Honor quite simply," said Miss Frayling.
"When Your Honor's learned colleague, Judge Bramcote, made
the order, he certainly had the mother's consent. But, if Your
Honor were to set aside the order and a fresh application
for an adoption order were made, Your Honor would certainly
not have her consent. I appear both for the natural father and
the mother, and I can assure Your Honor that the latter will

withdraw her consent as soon as she gets the opportunity."

"I see," said the judge. "Should that happen, I should then have to say that her consent was unreasonably withheld before I could make the order."

"Precisely," said Miss Frayling.

"Well, in that event," said the judge, "there still seems no point in taking two bites at this cherry. If you satisfy me on the evidence that in all the circumstances the child should go back to his natural parents, the application should be allowed and an adoption order refused. On the other hand, if, when I've heard the whole of the evidence, I'm satisfied that the mother's consent is unreasonably refused and that the putative father's objections should not prevail, your application to set aside the order should be dismissed."

"That, I agree, would be the effect, Your Honor," said Miss Frayling, "but, in the event of this case going further, I wish to insist on my client's strict legal rights. And one of these is, in my submission, that, provided Your Honor is satisfied he was under a legal liability to support the child, the adoption order should be set aside, whatever may happen thereafter."

"But surely," said the judge, "it must be a matter of discretion, even if you are correct in saying that your client was entitled to be served and it was through no fault of his that he was not served. An adoption order affects the status of the child. For all, or nearly all, legal purposes an adopted child becomes the child of Mr. and Mrs. A, instead of Mr. and Mrs. B. All sorts of things might have occurred as the result of the changed status of the child. Grave injustice might be done to people other than your client if the order were set aside, to people who were as innocent as your client. In such cases, surely the Court has an overriding discretion to decide whether the order should be set aside. I would have thought, subject to any argument of yours to the contrary, that the position would be the same as after a decree absolute of divorce. In such a case, a husband or wife who has not been served may apply to have the decree rescinded, but, though the Court *may* rescind it, it isn't bound to do so. In such cases, innocent people may be involved. The parties may have remarried, children may have been born, and so forth."

"Well, Your Honor," said Miss Frayling, "I see the force of Your Honor's argument. Fortunately for my client, nothing of the kind has happened in this case and I would respectfully submit that, if it is a matter of discretion, unless other innocent parties are affected, my client has a right that discretion should be exercised in his favor."

"You may be right," said the judge, "but the child is an innocent party, is he not? And he has certainly been affected, if only by living two years with Mr. and Mrs. Woodthorpe."

"There has been no further change of status, Your Honor."

"Does there have to be? The receipt of a fortune would not effect a change of legal status, but surely I should have to consider such a matter before rescinding an adoption order. The child is as innocent as your client. I should have thought that his situation was a matter relevant to the exercise of my discretion."

"Well, Your Honor," said Miss Frayling, "I will reserve further argument about the matter, as I hope to satisfy Your Honor in any event that, if it is a matter of discretion, it should be exercised in my client's favor."

"Very well then," said the judge. "You'd better call your evidence. But, first of all, I suppose, you should limit yourself to proving your client's liability under an agreement to support the child. Because, unless you prove that, that's an end of the matter. I gather that there are some distinguished medical gentlemen here. There's no point in their time being wasted in giving evidence if the application is to fail anyway."

"I agree, Your Honor," said Miss Frayling, "so I'll call Mr. West straightway."

Randolph took the oath and sat in the witness chair. In answer to Miss Frayling, he said he had paid for the expense of Hugh's birth, that he was abroad when the child was born but that, on returning to the country two months after the birth, he and Eleanor had lived together as husband and wife until he went to prison. He had paid for the child's maintenance from birth.

"I take it," said Mrs. Boulder, cross-examining, "that no affiliation order has ever been made against you, Mr. West?"

"It wasn't necessary," said Randolph.

"You simply kept the mother and child?"

"Exactly."

"Supposing you'd ceased to keep the mother—I'm not referring to the child for a moment—could she have sued you for failing to do so?"

"That would be for my lawyers to answer."

"As far as you know, were you liable to the mother under any kind of agreement to support her?"

"Not as far as I know."

"Now, coming to the child," said Mrs. Boulder, "your case is that you were liable under an agreement to support the child?"

"Yes."

"But you only supported the child in the same way as you supported the mother?"

"I suppose so."

"Nothing was said about your being liable to do so, or anything like that?"

"No, except once, in fun, she said she could get an order against me."

"She didn't mean it?"

"I'm sure she didn't intend to go to court about it. We were lovers, and she said it laughingly."

"Quite so. Then why do you say you were liable under an agreement to support the child? What agreement?"

"An agreement by my conduct in continuing to support the child."

"We're very legal, aren't we?" said Mrs. Boulder.

"Is that a question to the witness, Mrs. Boulder?" asked the judge.

Mrs. Boulder looked at the judge.

"I stand rebuked, Your Honor," she said. "But this conduct of yours, Mr. West," she went on, "was no different from your conduct in keeping the mother."

"There was this difference," said Randolph. "If I'd failed to keep her, she couldn't have sued me, but, if I'd failed to keep the child, she could have taken me to the police court and got an affiliation order against me."

"Mr. West," said Miss Frayling in re-examination, "will you tell His Honor a little more about this occasion when Miss Parton, or should I say Mrs. West, said she could get an order against you?"

"It's a little embarrassing," said Randolph.

"I'm afraid you'll have to overcome your embarrassment," said Miss Frayling. "Your answers might be important."

"Well," said Randolph, "we were in bed one night and we were teasing each other. She had done something to me, I'm not sure what—pulled my nose, or pinched me, or something—and I called her a little bastard. I'm afraid, Your Honor, that lovers do sometimes use language like that to each other, and even worse, purely in fun."

"I dare say," said the judge who, sitting so close to the parties and undistinguished by wig or gown, had difficulty in not showing slight embarrassment. His wife and he were very happily married. "I dare say," he repeated. "Go on, please."

"Well, when I called her that, she said: 'Not so much of your little bastard, or I'll be taking you to court about yours.' "

"Very well," said the judge. "What happened then?"

"Nothing, Your Honor," said Randolph. "I mean, nothing more was said on the subject."

"Thank you, Mr. West," said Miss Frayling. "Now, I have Mrs. West here who can corroborate Mr. West on this part of the case, but I don't think it's really in dispute. The question is whether an agreement by conduct has been proved. But, if my learned friend wants to cross-examine Mrs. West on this aspect of the case, I'll call her at once. I shall, of course, be calling on her later, if Your Honor decides this point in my favor."

Mrs. Boulder indicated that she did not want to cross-examine Eleanor on the point, and proceeded to address the judge.

"I suggest, Your Honor," she said, "that no agreement has been proved. It is true that Miss Parton, I beg your pardon, Mrs. West, could have gone to the Magistrate's Court if Mr. West had ceased to support the child, but could she have sued him in the County Court? In some cases the regular payment of money will establish a legal relationship, such as rent or payment for work done. But why should a payment by one lover to another create any legal relationship? I do not use the term lover offensively. I would say the same if they were husband and wife. A husband is normally bound to support his wife, and if he doesn't, she can make an application for maintenance in the Courts. But that doesn't mean that, if he's been regularly giving her, say, thirty pounds a week for maintenance and suddenly stops, she can sue him under an agreement to pay thirty pounds a week, unless they had made a binding agreement to this effect. And happily married people or people happily living together don't make such agreements—they don't need to."

"But, Mrs. Boulder," said the judge, "if the facts about this child and its mother and father had been brought to the notice of the Court, Mr. West would undoubtedly have been made a party to the case, wouldn't he?"

"Yes, Your Honor, I agree," said Mrs. Boulder, "but only because the Court would have said that he was a person who ought to be heard on the matter, not because he was liable under an agreement to support the child. As Your Honor knows, the Court has power to make any person it thinks proper a party to adoption proceedings. And I make a present of the fact to my learned friend that, if Your Honor had known the facts in this case, you wouldn't have troubled your head as to whether Mr. West was liable under an agreement; you would have said, 'Whether or not he is liable under an agreement to support the child, he ought to be made a party to the proceedings.' But, until Your Honor said that, he had no right to be served with the proceedings, and neither Your Honor nor Judge Bramcote said that, and the order was duly made. Consequently, although it may be hard on Mr. West, the fact that he would have been made a party to the proceedings if the facts had been known is irrelevant to this application, unless he had a *right* to be served with them. And he only had that right if he was liable under an agreement to support the child or if the Court had ordered him to be joined in the proceedings. In my respectful submission, neither of these conditions was fulfilled and this application should be dismissed."

"Your Honor," said Miss Frayling in reply. "Lovers and husbands and wives who are living happily together don't normally sign, seal and deliver deeds about their ordinary relationship. They don't put them into writing. They don't even expressly say, the one to the other, 'I agree to pay you so much a week for the child,' and the other to the one, 'I accept.' But they both know that an affiliation order can be obtained if the father does not support the child. And, in this case, we know from the jocular conversation in bed that both parties were well aware of the legal position. That being so, all that happens is all you'd expect to happen, namely that the father pays the mother so much a week."

"He didn't divide the amounts, I gather," said the judge. "He didn't say, 'Here is ten pounds for yourself and five pounds for Hugh.' He just handed over a lump sum?"

"That is true," said Miss Frayling. "But obviously a reasonable amount of that sum was intended for the support of the infant. Mrs. West accepted it. You don't require any particular form to make most kinds of agreement in this country. As my learned friend says, a person can go into a flat without any agreement, written or by word of mouth, and start paying rent. The amount of rent need not even have been agreed beforehand. If the landlord accepts it week by week, a tenancy is created. A dumb man could point out to a gardener his lawn and lawn mower. The gardener mows the lawn each Monday and is paid an amount each time. That would make an agreement by the one to employ the other to mow the lawn. Here the mother has a legal right to have the child maintained by the father, but there was, of course, a limit to the amount which the Court could allow. Many fathers would prefer to pay a larger sum than was legally necessary in order to avoid Court proceedings. In such a case, if the parties are on bad terms, they will have a written agreement. But if they are still lovers, no express agreement is necessary. In my submission, Mr. West has proved his case on this point and it would be a denial of justice if an innocent man who has suffered so much through no fault of his own should be deprived of the right at least to be heard on whether this order should be set aside.

"Should Your Honor dismiss this application at this stage, the position will be this. A man who was wrongly sent to prison will have been deprived of the right to be heard on the question whether his son should be taken away from him, partly through a false statement made by Mrs. West and partly, I must submit, through the casual way in which the adoption society, and the guardian, and, with the greatest respect and without intending to be impertinent, the Court itself dealt with the situation of the putative father. Having been deprived of that right when the adoption proceedings originally took place, he is now to be turned away from the judgment seat without being allowed to say a word. If that is the law, Your Honor, it certainly is not justice. And I feel sure that, in this Court, Your Honor would always wish justice to prevail if that is possible."

"That is so, I am sure, in every Court in this country, Miss Frayling," said the judge. "I don't think this preliminary point is at all an easy one. Although I originally said I should decide it first, I shall exercise a privilege which is said to belong to the learned advocates in this case, and change my mind. I shall hear the whole case before giving a decision on any part of it."

So Randolph was recalled into the witness box. First of all, he told how he had met Eleanor, and said that it was only after the child's birth that he had fallen in love with her. It was only two months after the child's birth that he went to live with Eleanor and she became known as Mrs. West. He described their year of happiness. He then dealt with his arrest, conviction and pardon. He also spoke in moving terms and with some emotion of his love for Hugh, and of his desperate wish to have him back. No one in the room could have failed to be touched by his obvious sincerity.

Mrs. Boulder then began to cross-examine him.

"Mr. West," she began, "we all know that in certain respects you are a very wronged man. Please don't think that I haven't that well in mind when I ask you some very unpleasant questions."

"Thank you," said Randolph.

"You have complained at not being served with these proceedings, but initially that's your fault, isn't it?"

"For giving a child to Miss Parton, I agree. I've admitted that already."

"I'm not referring to that," said Mrs. Boulder, "but to your conduct after you knew she was going to have a child."

"I paid all the expenses."

"You paid all the expenses," repeated Mrs. Boulder. "Yes, you paid all the expenses. You were a grown man, you had amused yourself at a girl's expense and got her in the family way. Did you think your responsibility consisted solely in paying the expenses?"

"What else could I have done?"

"Did you consider at the time what else you could have done?"

"I don't know that I did."

"Well, perhaps you'd consider it now," said Mrs. Boulder. "Did you ask the girl whether she'd like you to come and live with her?"

"No."

"Later you did live with her?"

"Yes."

"And she changed her name to West?"

"Yes."

"You now wish to marry her after you are free?"

"Definitely."

"Now, if you'd gone to live with her before the child was born, and she'd changed her name before its birth, it could have had both your names on the birth certificate."

"That is so."

"If you'd done that, the child could never have been put out for adoption without your knowing it, could it?"

"I suppose not."

"Then whose fault was it initially that no one asked you whether you agreed to the adoption?"

"Isn't that for me to say?" interposed the judge. "It doesn't matter what the view of the witness is, does it? What we want from the witness are the facts."

"If Your Honor pleases," said Mrs. Boulder. "Well now, Mr. West, you never even considered whether it would be for the benefit of the child if you went to live with the mother?"

"I didn't intend to marry her at the time."

"That's frank, at any rate," said Mrs. Boulder, "but it doesn't show much consideration for your child, does it?"

"If you put it that way."

"How would you put it?" asked Mrs. Boulder.

"It wouldn't have done anyone any good for me to go and live with Eleanor unless we loved each other."

"It might have done the child some good. After all, you had been ready enough to sleep with the girl for your own purposes. You wouldn't have bound yourself to anything by going to live with her. You could always have left later and the child would have had the advantage of having two names on the birth certificate."

"She could have done that, anyway."

"Really, Mr. West," said Mrs. Boulder, "are you seriously suggesting that a girl should change her name to that of a man she'd met once at a dance?"

"It would be quite a good idea," said the judge, "from the point of view of the child. If, later on, the two people did marry, that would be fine. If they did not, the birth certificate would look no worse than one with a blank in the column for the father's name. It would show Eleanor West as the mother and Randolph West as the father. The fact that the addresses were different might only suggest that the parties were living apart at the time of the birth. The child would appear legitimate. As it is, all that appears on the certificate is Eleanor Parton, mother, and no father."

"Did you suggest to Miss Parton that she should change her name before you went to live with her?"

"No."

"Then you can't very well blame her for not thinking of it."

"Of course, I don't blame her."

"But you never even tried to think if there was anything else you could do for the boy, besides paying for him to be brought into the world and to stay in it?"

"If I'd realized everything that was going to happen, I might have acted differently."

"I dare say, but, as it was, you considered your responsibility was discharged by paying money, like a man with a discarded mistress?"

"I don't like that way of putting it."

"I dare say you don't," said Mrs. Boulder, "but it's an apt comparison, isn't it? All you were going to do was pay."

"I think you've made that point sufficiently, Mrs. Boulder," said the judge, intervening. "But, as we're on the subject, I'm not at all sure that even in this day and age a man should stand in danger of losing his rights at law because he doesn't go and live in sin with a woman. It is still immoral and contrary to religious teaching to do so. Yet at the end of this case, when I'm weighing the rights and wrongs of the matter, you are going to ask me to put in the scales against Mr. West that he didn't go and live with Miss Parton sooner than he did. Does adultery improve with its continuance?"

"In cases where marriage is impossible, it may well be that it does, Your Honor," said Mrs. Boulder.

"Why not wait till marriage *is* possible? Why oughtn't Mr. West to have waited until he could get a divorce, before going to live with Miss Parton?"

"If that had been his reason," said Mrs. Boulder, "if he had said that he was ashamed of his one act of adultery and did not propose to repeat it, one could have respected such an attitude. But that was not at all the case with Mr. West. As soon as he found that he loved Miss Parton or, as I might say more unkindly, wanted to sleep with her again, and she was available for the purpose, he went to live with her. No moral scruples there, Your Honor."

"Quite right, Mrs. Boulder," said the judge, "but I'll still want a lot of convincing that the fact that a man did not go and live in adultery is to be held against him in a Court of Law."

Mrs. Boulder concluded her cross-examination. Miss Frayling did not re-examine, and Eleanor was then called. In answer to Miss Frayling, she gave the history of her association with Randolph, of the birth of the child and of her putting him out for adoption. She ended by saying that she wanted the child back.

Mrs. Boulder's first question was:

"Is it you or Mr. West who wants the child back more?"

"We both want him."

"Equally?"

A slight hesitation, then: "Yes," said Eleanor.

"Quite sure?"

"As far as I can tell."

"You gave your consent to the adoption freely?"

"I did. I was in a terrible state at the time. Randolph was in prison for years. He might have been a sexual maniac."

"It was your own decision? No one tried to persuade you?"

"No."

"It was you all along who wanted the child to be adopted?"

"Yes. It was a dreadful position to be in. I did what I thought was right."

"You thought it right to lie to the authorities?"

"I had to. Mr. West would never have agreed."

"So you deceived everyone?"

"Yes. Which is the worse—to lie or to give a baby no fair chance in life? That was my problem. There *are* worse things than telling lies, Your Honor, and, in my view, to have kept Hugh in the circumstances would have been one of them. Sometimes it must be right to lie and I still think I was right in this case to do so."

"But, as a result of your deception, my clients have brought this child up as their own for two years, whereas, if you'd told the truth, that wouldn't have happened."

"I know. I'm more sorry than I can say. But I couldn't tell what was going to happen, could I? Of course, I wouldn't have let Hugh go if I had had any idea that Randolph would be pardoned."

"Your regrets wouldn't be much consolation to Mr. and Mrs. Woodthorpe if they lost the child now, would they?"

"I suppose not."

"Have you considered at all the effect upon the child if you have him back?"

"Of course I have."

"And what effect d'you think it will have?"

"He may be unhappy for a time, but we *are* his real parents and he *was* with us for a year, and I think he will soon get used to us again, and be happy."

"Supposing an eminent psychiatrist were to say that it might be dangerous for the child to return to you, would that alter your view?"

"In what way dangerous?"

"Supposing he just said dangerous?"

"Then I'd ask him what he meant by it."

Mrs. Boulder smiled.

"You're quite right," she said. "Supposing he said that the boy might develop serious neuroses when he grew older?"

"I'm told that this may happen to any child, however brought up."

"But if you were told by a doctor you trusted that to take this child back might give it a greater chance of suffering from a neurosis than if he stayed where he was, would that change your mind about asking for the child back?"

"If I believed that the child would come to harm by returning to us, I should not ask for this to be done. But it would take more than one doctor to make me believe this, even if he were a doctor whom I trusted. I trust my dentist, but he has sometimes hurt me unnecessarily. At least, I believe it was unnecessary. If every doctor said the same, that would be different. But we are calling a doctor who says that Hugh is unlikely to come to any harm if he comes back to us."

"Now, of course, you've talked this matter over with Mr. West?"

"Naturally."

"There seems no doubt at all that Mr. West is desperately attached to the child?"

"That is absolutely true."

"He would do anything legal to get the child back?"

"Certainly."

"Have you ever talked over with him the possible danger to the child of having him back?"

"Yes, I have."

"Who raised the question first, you or he?"

Eleanor hesitated. "I couldn't be sure. I think *I* did."

"And what was his reaction?"

"That everything would be all right."

"That was his immediate reaction when this question arose?"

"Yes."

"Was it yours?"

"I agreed with him."

"Immediately?"

"We discussed the matter, and I agreed with him."

"Well then, if it was you who first raised the matter, you must have had some doubt about it?"

"It naturally occurred to me, and I thought it right to talk about it to Randolph."

"Would it be right to say, then, that before this application was made, you wondered whether it would be good for the boy to have him back?"

"Yes."

"And you then mentioned it to Mr. West?"

"Yes."

"Are you sure of this?"

"Yes."

"Quite sure?"

"Yes."

"Then why, when I asked you who first raised this question, did you say: 'I can't be sure. I think *I* did.' "

"I wasn't sure then, but I am now. I don't suppose you've ever been in a witness box, Mrs. Boulder. It's not easy to be sure on the spur of the moment."

"Very well then," said Mrs. Boulder, "will you tell me this? Mr. West will be heartbroken if this application fails. Will you?"

"I shall be terribly upset."

"But not as upset as Mr. West?"

"I haven't had two years in prison, dreaming of a child who wasn't there."

"And whose fault were those dreams?"

"Mine," said Eleanor, "but I think I was right at the time. I tried to believe in Randolph's innocence but how could I be sure? Twelve impartial people were sure of his guilt."

"I asked you if you would be as upset as Mr. West would be, if this application failed. You didn't answer directly, but do I rightly assume from your answer that you would not be as upset as he would be?"

"That is true," said Eleanor, "but you must understand that I underwent my ordeal two years ago, when I gave Hugh away. I was heartbroken then. And it was a terrible ordeal to have to pretend he was still with me. But one does somehow get used to things. I shall be most unhappy if Hugh does not come back to us. I loved him dearly, and still do. I shall be even more unhappy because of the pain to Randolph after all he has suffered already."

"Do you think you will suffer more than Mr. and Mrs. Woodthorpe if the boy they dote on is suddenly snatched from them?"

"I know of no way of measuring suffering," said Eleanor. "Two people are going to be made desperately unhappy by the order in this case."

"It could be three, couldn't it?" said Mrs. Boulder. "You've forgotten Hugh."

And, like a good dramatist, Mrs. Boulder made that her exit line. Miss Frayling did not re-examine, and called her next witness.

This was Dr. Bream, a psychiatrist. In order to give the doctors an opportunity of meeting Hugh without upsetting him or making him self-conscious, it had been arranged that there should be a tea party at the Woodthorpes', which they attended. They were thus able to see him in his normal surroundings and casually ask him anything which they thought might be of value.

Dr. Bream took the oath and sat in the witness chair. First he gave a list of his qualifications. They were impressive.

"Dr. Bream," asked Miss Frayling, "before I ask you about the particular boy in this case, I should like to ask you some general questions."

"By all means."

"Generally speaking, is it better for a child to be in the same home until it is grown up?"

"That depends on the home, Madam," said the doctor.

"Dr. Bream," said the judge, "you are used to giving evidence, I believe?"

"Indeed, yes, Your Honor."

"Then no doubt you are used to listening to the question before you answer it?"

"Of course, Your Honor."

"Did you not hear Miss Frayling say 'generally speaking' in her question?"

"I did, Your Honor."

"Then did you not realize from that expression that Miss Frayling was excluding cases where the father came home drunk every night or the mother took drugs? She was referring to the ordinary decent household in this country, households where psychiatrists are never required."

Although Dr. Bream had laid himself open to this attack, he was not taking the very last of the judge's remarks without a fight.

"Your Honor would be surprised at the number of households where our services are required. Unfortunately, we are often not sent for, with lamentable results."

"Indeed?" said the judge. "Now would you be kind enough to answer Miss Frayling's question. Perhaps you'd repeat it, Miss Frayling?"

"No need, thank you," said Dr. Bream. "I remember it perfectly. And the answer is 'yes.' "

"But I've forgotten the question," said the judge. "So 'yes' means nothing to me."

"Generally speaking," said Dr. Bream, slightly emphasizing the words. "Generally speaking," he repeated, "it is better for a child to be brought up in one home."

"It hardly requires your eminent services to tell us that," said the judge.

"I was asked the question," said Dr. Bream, "and I understand that it is contempt of Court not to answer."

"It is also contempt of Court to try to be funny in the witness box, Dr. Bream," said the judge. "Now, let's get on, Miss Frayling."

"Have you known many cases of children who, for one reason or another, have changed from one home to another at an early age, say the age of three or thereabouts?"

"Yes, I have," said Dr. Bream.

"What percentage of these children have, in your view, suffered in any way from the change?"

"I can't be dogmatic about it, but I should say about fifty per cent."

"So it is an even chance," asked the judge, "that a child who changes its home at the age of three will suffer in consequence?"

"I didn't say so, Your Honor."

"Did you not say 'about fifty per cent'?"

"Certainly."

"That's an even chance."

"It is, Your Honor."

"Then why do you say to me that you didn't say it was an

even chance that a child who changes its home at the age of
three will suffer in consequence?"

"Because I didn't say it, Your Honor."

"Really, Doctor, perhaps I'm in need of your attention, but
you have made two completely opposite statements."

"No," said Dr. Bream, "I have not."

"Let me try again," said the judge. "Did you not say fifty
per cent, and is that not an even chance?"

"Certainly, Your Honor."

"But now you say you didn't say it."

"I did say that, Your Honor."

"Then you agree that fifty per cent of children who are
moved from one home to another at the age of three suffer in
consequence?"

"No, Your Honor. I did not say it and I do not believe it
to be true."

"Miss Frayling, would you be good enough to elucidate?"
said the judge.

"I think," began Miss Frayling, "that what the doctor
means . . ."

But Mrs. Boulder interrupted.

"I should be obliged if the doctor will tell us himself what
he means without being led by Miss Frayling."

"Very well, Dr. Bream," said Miss Frayling, "will you tell
the learned judge what you meant?"

"It's quite simple," said Dr. Bream. "I said that about fifty
per cent of the children whose cases I've known about have
suffered through a change of home at an early age."

The judge pushed his papers away from him in a gesture of
annoyance. In fact, he pushed them so far that Miss Frayling
had very delicately to push them back again, or they would have
become confused with her own.

"That is exactly what *I* said," said the judge. "And we've wasted five minutes getting there."

"But with respect, Your Honor," said Dr. Bream, "it is not what you said."

"I may or may not be in need of your services, Doctor, but I am quite capable of remembering what I said a few minutes ago."

"I'm very sorry to be persistent," said Dr. Bream, "but Your Honor said that I had said that fifty per cent of children moved at an early age from one home to another suffer in consequence."

"And you have just admitted that you said that."

"I have not, Your Honor. I have agreed that fifty per cent of the children *whose cases I have known about* have suffered from a change of home. Many of the children I see are not normal children, anyway. About half of these children have suffered, as I've said. But I wouldn't at all agree that anything like that percentage of normal children would suffer."

"I see," said the judge, and remained silent for some time.

"What is your opinion of the likelihood of a normal child being injuriously affected by a change of home at the age of three?"

"Given a similar kind of home with similar standards and fond parents or foster parents, I would say that very few normal children would come to any harm. I have had a case or two where the only definite fact we could ascertain was a change of environment at an early age, but we could only guess that that was the cause of the trouble. It might have been something quite else. For a normal child, given the good conditions which I've mentioned, the risk of injury is very small indeed, far less than the risk of being run over in the streets or injured by accident at home."

"Of course, if a child is not normal, different consideration will apply?"

"Naturally."

"Or if the home to which it is sent is in certain respects unsatisfactory?"

"Agreed."

"Now, you have seen this child once. Did you see enough of it to be able to say whether it is normal or not?"

"'Well, I was told by Mr. and Mrs. Woodthorpe's doctor that physically he was absolutely normal. On that basis and from what I observed myself, I would say unquestionably that Hugh is a normal, happy child."

"Have you talked to Mr. and Mrs. West, to see what sort of people they are?"

"I have. I have interviewed them for a total period of five-and-a-half hours. On different occasions, of course."

"And what sort of people did you find them?"

"They have a high standard mentally. They seem to me to be well-balanced, kind people, who would give an admirable home to any child. Mr. West is undoubtedly very strung-up at these proceedings. It would be strange if he were not. I was, however, much impressed by his self-control. Many normal men who had undergone his hardships and continued strain would not have stood up to them anything like as well as he has."

"In your opinion, Dr. Bream," asked Miss Frayling, "if Hugh goes back to his natural parents, is there any likelihood that he will have a less happy or useful life than if he stays where he is?"

"In my opinion," said Dr. Bream, "there is not."

"Thank you, Dr. Bream," said Miss Frayling. "That is all I wish to ask."

"Dr. Bream," asked Mrs. Boulder, "are you always as confident of your opinions as you appear to be in this case?"

"Certainly not. Sometimes I am far from confident."

"You have given evidence in a good many cases, have you not?"

"I have."

"Have you given evidence in cases where you felt far from confident?"

"Quite possibly."

"When giving evidence in such cases have you, nevertheless, appeared to be confident?"

"Like counsel, d'you mean?" said Dr. Bream, and, like Oscar Wilde when he joked in cross-examination, immediately regretted it. He realized what was coming and it came.

"Yes," said Mrs. Boulder, "like counsel."

Dr. Bream hesitated. If he agreed that expert witnesses were very like counsel, he would be admitting that he was an advocate rather than a witness. The certainty with which he had given his evidence would be discounted accordingly. Counsel are entitled to appear to have a firm belief in the righteousness of their client's cause, provided they make no false statement in the process. If he said expert witnesses were not at all like counsel, he would be asked why he raised the matter. And, confound it, he *had* raised the matter. After a little more thought, he decided that there was only one way out. Otherwise, he could see Mrs. Boulder neatly folding him up and tying the string around him as though he were a brown paper parcel.

"I'm sorry, Mrs. Boulder," he said, "I was joking."

Mrs. Boulder looked at him, paused for a moment and then said rather than asked:

"You were joking."

"I'm afraid so."

"I see," said Mrs. Boulder. "This is a case where both parties are suffering a tremendous strain and where one side or the other is going to suffer great distress, and you thought it right in answer to one of my very first questions to make a joke."

"I shouldn't have done so."

"Perhaps you would tell me whether there were any other jokes in your evidence?"

"No, there were not. I repeat, I'm sorry about that one."

Mrs. Boulder, like the good bulldog she was, considered whether to have another bite at this particularly juicy piece of Dr. Bream, or whether to try somewhere else. She decided not to spoil her first mouthful.

"Then perhaps we may return to the question, Dr. Bream. In some cases where you have given evidence, but have been far from confident, have you appeared to be confident in giving your evidence?"

"I have tried to tell the truth."

"Successfully, Dr. Bream?" queried Mrs. Boulder.

"I hope so."

"No doubt, Dr. Bream, but would you now mind answering my question directly?"

"I thought I had."

Dr. Bream was not enjoying himself. This bulldog showed every sign of not just nipping him round the ankle joints but of making a pretty good meal of him.

"I asked you if you had appeared confident in certain cases."

"How can I tell how I appear to other people?" asked Dr. Bream.

Mrs. Boulder made a gesture of pushing away her papers from her, much as the judge had done. One of the disadvantages for advocates at hearings in a judge's private room is that the advocate remains seated while questioning the witness, and cannot therefore drop his papers on the desk as a gesture of impatience. But Mrs. Boulder's substitute was quite effective.

"I rather prefer your jokes to your hedging, Dr. Bream," she said.

them to the dog, in the hope that it would leave his flesh alone.

"Have any of your other answers been stupid?"

"That is not for me to say."

"But it is, Doctor," persisted Mrs. Boulder, flinging his discarded pants contemptuously aside. "You yourself have described one of your answers as stupid. I want to know if you'd describe any of your other answers as stupid. Would you?"

"No."

"None?"

"No."

"What about the joke?" asked Mrs. Boulder, putting her paw on the old wound just to keep it smarting.

"Yes, that was stupid. I'd forgotten."

"You'd forgotten about the joke, Dr. Bream?" asked Mrs. Boulder incredulously.

"Well, not forgotten," said Dr. Bream. "I hadn't got it in mind."

"Well, bearing it in mind, Dr. Bream, you have made two stupid answers in your evidence?"

"Yes."

"D'you usually make two stupid answers when you are giving evidence, Dr. Bream?"

"I don't think so."

"But you have today?"

"Yes."

"Would it be unfair to say, then, that you are being more than usually stupid in giving your evidence today?"

"Isn't that just being offensive, Mrs. Boulder?" said the judge.

"Perhaps, Your Honor," said Mrs. Boulder, "but I do want to know if the doctor's having an off-day. If he is, his evidence can't count for very much, in my submission."

The doctor decided to launch a counterattack.

"I've never been cross-examined so offensively," he said.

"I don't think you should talk to the witness like t[...]
Boulder," said the judge. "Your right and duty is to [...]
tions, not to be offensive."

"I'm sorry, Your Honor," said Mrs. Boulder.

The witness was grateful for the respite. He was not [...]
being mauled about in the very first round.

"Dr. Bream," said Mrs. Boulder, "I apologize for be[...]
fensive, but do you not agree that every professional ad[...]
witness or speaker must know perfectly well whether he [...]
ing an appearance of confidence when he speaks?"

"I suppose that is right."

"Then why did you say to me, 'How can I tell how I a[...]
to other people?' "

"Well, I can't be sure what impression I make on an [...]
ence."

"Of course not, but you can be sure whether you've [...]
yourself justice, made a good show, put your point across [...]
or however you like to put it?"

"Yes, I suppose so."

"Then, when I asked you whether you appeared confiden[...]
certain cases when you gave evidence, why did you answ[...]
'How can I tell how I appear to other people?' "

"Well, it wasn't a very good answer."

"Was it a joke or a hedge? I don't mean that question [...]
fensively. I want to know the answer."

"It was certainly not a joke."

"Then was it a hedge?"

"I hope I never hedge."

"Then it couldn't have been a hedge?"

"No."

"Then what was it? An honest answer?"

"An honest but stupid answer."

Dr. Bream was beginning to take off his clothes and hand[...]

"I see," said Mrs. Boulder. "So your stupid answers were due to offensive questions, were they?"

"They were asked offensively," said Dr. Bream.

"Let us see," said Mrs. Boulder, of whom Mr. Luttrell had rightly said that, when she got her teeth into anything, she wouldn't let go. "The first stupid answer you gave was in answer to my question: 'When giving evidence in such cases have you, nevertheless, appeared to be confident?' What was offensive about the question?"

Dr. Bream began to regret his impetuosity. He handed a sock to his opponent.

"No, that question was not offensive."

Mrs. Boulder did not even sniff the sock.

"Was my manner in asking it offensive?"

"I can't say that it was."

"Then your first stupid answer was not due to the offensiveness of my question?"

"Apparently not."

"But you said it was."

"That was a mistake."

"Would it be fair to describe it as a stupid mistake?"

"No doubt you think so, Mrs. Boulder."

The dog opened its mouth wide preparatory to tasting a large piece of Dr. Bream.

"It doesn't matter what I think," said Mrs. Boulder, "but do you not, Dr. Bream," she asked with quiet emphasis, "deeply regret having made that answer?"

There was little fight left in the doctor.

"Yes, I'm sorry I said it."

"And are you not sorry because it was a stupid thing to say?"

"I suppose so."

"So we now have three stupid answers. I take it that is most unusual, Dr. Bream?"

"Yes."

"Can you account for them? Perhaps you're not feeling quite yourself?"

"I have been working rather hard."

"No doubt much too hard, Doctor. I sympathize. Perhaps you'd prefer the learned judge not to take too much notice of your evidence, if you feel that on this occasion you haven't done yourself justice?"

"Not in answer to *your* questions."

"So you'd like the learned judge to pay regard to your examination-in-chief but not to your cross-examination?"

"Does it matter what the doctor wants? Have you much more to ask the witness?" said the judge. He felt like stopping the fight. The doctor was taking too much punishment.

"I have some more questions, Your Honor," said Mrs. Boulder, "and one of them is one of my early ones which still remains unanswered. In cases where you were not confident, Doctor, have you not given evidence as though you were?"

"In every case I have given my honest opinion."

"Confidently, or not?"

"As confidently as the nature of the case allowed," said Dr. Bream.

Why didn't I think of that answer before? he asked himself.

"That means that, when you did not feel confident about a matter, you made it plain in your evidence that you were not confident about it?"

"Precisely."

"Now, this is not intended as an offensive question, Doctor, but you were paid to give such evidence?"

"Yes."

"Quite well paid?"

"My normal fees."

"Which are not inconsiderable?"

"Must I answer such questions, Your Honor?" The doctor appealed to the judge.

"I really don't see why you should," said the judge.

"Very well," said Mrs. Boulder. "Can you think of any reason in the world why a party to proceedings should pay you your usual fees to get you to give evidence that you were not at all confident in your opinion? That wouldn't be worth much, would it?"

"I didn't get up and say I wasn't confident in what I was saying."

"But your manner and expressions or both showed that you weren't confident. That is what you've just said. 'As confidently as the nature of the case allowed.' And you agreed that you made it plain in your evidence that you were not confident in the matter. How did you make it plain except by your manner or what you said?"

Dr. Bream no longer congratulated himself on this answer. He hadn't thought of it before because it was a rotten answer.

"I can't recall every case I've given evidence in," he said lamely.

The dog sniffed and looked at the torn clothing and the mauled, naked body of the doctor. There was no need to bite any more for the moment. Mrs. Boulder decided that a little astringent lotion applied to the wounds might do no harm.

"Dr. Bream, I expect you know Dr. Crestway, whom I shall be calling as a witness?"

Unfortunately, Mrs. Boulder's first choice, Dr. Baldry, had been taken ill, while Dr. Mallet was at a conference in America. So they had to risk Crestway. Having regard to the treatment Dr. Bream had received, Dr. Crestway looked a good bet, she thought, and then shivered. Bet, she had said. Mustn't mention anything like that to Dr. Crestway.

"Yes, I know Dr. Crestway," said Dr. Bream.

"He disagrees entirely about the effect of moving children of three from one home to another."

"We often disagree," said Dr. Bream.

"But he is an eminent psychiatrist?"

"Certainly."

"You have often heard him give evidence?"

"Yes, frequently."

"And sometimes you have given evidence on opposite sides, as you are doing today? Was Dr. Crestway always wrong when he disagreed with you?"

"I thought so, naturally."

"Why 'naturally'? We're all fallible. He might have convinced you that you were wrong. I take it that you are open to argument? Of course, you might convince him that he was wrong or vice versa?"

"Yes."

"So you were open to being convinced by him that you were wrong?"

"Certainly."

"Then why did you say, when I asked you if Dr. Crestway was always wrong when he disagreed with you, 'I thought so, *naturally*'?"

"Because I thought he was wrong."

"Why did you use the word 'naturally'?"

"I'm not sure."

"It slipped out, didn't it? It meant that he was an advocate on one side and you were the advocate on the other and so *naturally* you didn't agree."

"If you say so."

"But d'you agree?"

"I suppose so."

"Well, which did you mean, Doctor? Do you mean that, when you give evidence in a case, you give your honest opinion and are prepared to admit that it is wrong if other evidence convinces you of that, or do you mean that, when you give evidence, you are going to back up the side you are fighting for and are *naturally* not going to alter your evidence?"

"I shouldn't have used the word 'naturally.'"

"Perhaps not, Dr. Bream, but you did. Was that another stupid answer?"

Dr. Bream did not answer, but the dog was satisfied and subsided, licking its lips.

"Any re-examination, Miss Frayling?" asked the judge.

"Dr. Bream," asked Miss Frayling, "my learned friend in asking you questions has, as far as I can recollect, asked you not a single question about this boy. Having heard her questions, are you still of the same opinion of the effect on the boy of being given back to his real parents?"

"I am," said Dr. Bream, and thankfully withdrew.

"That is the case for Mr. West," said Miss Frayling.

First Mary and then Bill gave evidence. They told how and why they came to adopt Hugh, of their great fondness for him, of his progress as a child and of the desperate unhappiness Mary in particular would suffer if they lost him.

When they had completed their evidence, Dr. Crestway was called. In answer to Mrs. Boulder, he said, among other things:

"We are born, Your Honor, with certain physical characteristics which can be developed or neglected but which can never be radically altered. Great sportsmen are born, not made. It is quite true that many people have physical characteristics which, if carefully and painstakingly developed, will result in their being, for example, better at a particular game than many of their fellows. But they will never be champions unless they start with the necessary physical equipment. The same applies to the brain. Unless a baby is born with the necessary mental equipment, it will never reach the highest ranks with its brain.

Fellows of All Souls are born, not made. Of course, you can get borderline cases with brain or body. In such cases, extra development may compensate for the initial slight inferiority. But to be a top-class athlete or a Fellow of All Souls you must start with a certain minimum of physical or mental equipment, as the case may be. Without that minimum, no training, no teaching will produce the desired result. So my first premise is that you cannot change the brain or the body. You can only improve the material already there."

"I can understand that," said the judge, "and it sounds logical, but I don't at the moment see how it is going to help me in this case."

"Your Honor will," said Dr. Crestway. "I have said that you cannot change the brain or the body. But each human being consists of more than brain and body. I am not speaking from a religious point of view when I say that every baby born into the world has a soul. You may call it personality or psyche, if you wish, but it is just as much a part of the person as his brain or body. But there is a very great difference between the personality, as I prefer to call it, on the one hand, and the body and brain on the other. The latter cannot be changed, the former can be. In the first years of a child's life—the Jesuits say up till seven; I would not be so dogmatic about the exact age, which might be only five or six or even less in some cases, and as late as eight in a few others—in those first years the personality is developed and may be changed this way or that. All sorts of things may happen to it which can have the most appalling consequences both to the child and to the people with whom it comes in contact in later life. Delicate as are the brain and the nervous system, the personality is an even more delicate part of our equipment. Medical science is not yet sufficiently advanced to show how and why the personality can be changed or affected, but it is as true to say that it *can* be changed or affected as it is to say that the brain can be injured by a knock on the head."

The witness paused. "I hope I have made myself clear," he said.

"Perfectly," said the judge.

"Well now," went on Dr. Crestway, "given an ordinary normal baby, brought up in an ordinary normal way, the brain and body will come to no harm. But the delicate mechanism of the personality is such that, without anyone appreciating the fact, much harm can be done to a child's personality with lasting effects. Those effects may range from the merely inconvenient to the disastrous. Unfortunately, we are not able to produce a book of rules which will tell parents how to ensure that their child's personality is not adversely affected by its upbringing. But there is no doubt that one apparently trifling experience can affect a child for life. One word spoken, one sight seen, and I am not referring to dramatic matters at all, but to such everyday occurrences as an angry word spoken by a man to his wife—complete strangers to the child—or a mild slap given to another child who had been naughty. Everything a child sees or hears or otherwise experiences goes to the formation or alteration of its personality. I hope I am still being lucid, Your Honor."

"I am enjoying your lecture, Doctor," said the judge.

"Now, there are many unfortunate people today who, as far as one can tell, are sound in brain and body but who suffer from neuroses of various kinds. These neuroses are sometimes comparatively innocuous but sometimes very grave indeed. Many of them are, in my opinion, a result of some experience of the adult during his formative years as a child. I have had apparently normal people in my care who, if they were in a house, could not go out of it. Or, if they were outside, could not go in. Such unfortunate people are often highly intelligent and will tell me that their fear of going out of the house, or into it, as the case might be, is quite irrational. They know that no harm will come to them, and yet they have this desperate fear which makes them break out into a sweat and have a feeling of grave panic at the mere idea of stepping outside the front door. And this on a beautiful, peaceful day, when they know that no harm can come to them.

"These patients of mine come from every class of society, from those qualified to be Fellows of All Souls and from those who failed, and rightly, to pass their eleven-plus exams. The exact cause of these neuroses, which precipitate utter misery in the patients, in spite of the fact that they know there is no physical reason for them, we do not know. But we do know that their origin is something to do with the patients' personalities. It must be. We can see that mind and body are sound. There is only one other part of a human being which can be sick. And we know this too, that sometimes the cause of this sickness is to be found in an early experience or early experiences of the patient as a child.

"Now, I have said that we can produce no books of rules to give to parents to enable them to bring up their children without injury to their personality. But we do know this. It is obvious, is it not, that violent action in a child's life should be avoided, if possible? I am not, of course, referring to physical violence, but to things like violent change. Such as, for example, a change of home. In some cases a change of home cannot be avoided. Both parents might be killed in an accident or the like. Indeed, I had a patient not long ago whose parents were killed in an air crash when she was four. She was brought up by a most kindly aunt and uncle and appears to have had as happy a childhood as was possible in the circumstances. But I have no doubt that the illness for which I was treating her was due to the appalling wrench suffered by the child's personality by her change of home. I am quite satisfied in my own mind that, unless it is unavoidable, the home of a child of tender years should never be changed."

"What d'you say about this particular child?" asked Mrs. Boulder, who was very happy to have let the doctor have his head, so long as the judge did not appear restive.

"I have seen the child, the parents and the adopters. If I may say so, they all appear admirably normal. I cannot, of course, say what harm may have already been done to the child by the wrench to its personality when its home was changed at the age of one. Let us hope he will be lucky. But, in my view, to give his personality another wrench by another change at the age of three would be a very wrong thing to do, very wrong indeed. If it were necessary, it would, of course, have to be done, but I have no hesitation in saying that it would be most undesirable and may have deplorable results on the child in later years. I should make it plain that what I am saying reflects in no way on the home which the real parents wish to provide. As far as loving care and good sense are concerned, I am sure that it would be an admirable home—for any child but this. No home would be admirable for this boy except the one he at present enjoys."

"Thank you, Doctor," said Mrs. Boulder, and Miss Frayling began to cross-examine.

"You disagree with Dr. Bream, I gather?"

"I do."

"But do you think the child may be quite all right when he grows up, if he's left where he is?"

"I certainly hope so."

"There is a reasonable chance of it?"

"Yes, there is a reasonable chance."

"In spite of the first change?"

"I've already said so."

"Then you can't be sure, Doctor, that harm would come from a further change?"

"I cannot, of course, guarantee it, but a change at the age of three is more violent than a change at the earlier age. And for a child to be played about with like a shuttlecock appears to me to be highly undesirable. There are enough risks in life without imposing that on him."

"But you must have known adults who, through some such accident as you mentioned, became orphans at an early age and who suffer from no neuroses?"

"That is so, but why take the risk?"

"Doctor," said Miss Frayling, "I'd be grateful if you'd just answer my questions instead of questioning me. You have known quite normal people who were orphaned at an early age?"

"Yes, but none who were orphaned twice. None whose parents died when they were one and whose foster parents died when they were three."

"Presumably there are such people in the world."

"I should imagine so."

"But none of them patients of yours?"

"No."

"So, for all you know, none of these twice-orphaned children have come to any harm—in the way of neuroses, I mean."

"As I don't know of any such case, I cannot say what their history has been."

"Of course not. I imagine that you talk about cases to your colleagues; not by way of chitchat, I mean, but seriously for the benefit of everyone generally?"

"Of course."

"In your time you must have had a good many colleagues?"

"Certainly."

"Has any one of your colleagues ever mentioned to you a case of a twice-orphaned child who subsequently became a victim of a neurosis?"

"I shouldn't be surprised."

"Can you recall a single instance?"

"I can't say that I can."

"So that, as far as your evidence goes, you have not had experience yourself of a patient who was twice-orphaned as a child, and you know no one else who has?"

"I tell you, I can't recall."

"Then it follows that you are not able to say that any such child has come to any harm in later years from a neurosis?"

"I think it very likely that such children have so suffered."

"But that is surmise, Doctor."

"Surmise, but based on knowledge of human psychology in its widest sense."

"What would you say the odds would be?"

"The odds?" repeated the doctor sharply—and Mrs. Boulder felt slight apprehension.

"Yes," said Miss Frayling, "the odds on Hugh turning out all right if he goes back to his parents."

The doctor hesitated, and began to look slightly like a horse being led quietly around the paddock when he suddenly sees someone he doesn't like.

"Is it an even chance that he'll be all right, or two to one or ten to one against, or what?"

The doctor still said nothing, but Mrs. Boulder sadly imagined that she could see the whites of his eyes and that he might buck at any moment.

"Put it in terms of percentages, if you prefer," said Miss Frayling, and Mrs. Boulder made a mental note to thank her opponent afterward.

"I should *very much* prefer to put it in terms of percentages," said the doctor so vehemently that Miss Frayling could not resist asking why.

"Because I don't like references to odds in any shape or form," said the doctor quite fiercely.

The judge looked puzzled, and Miss Frayling decided that the matter was worth pursuing.

"What's the objection, Doctor?" she asked, and Mrs. Boulder feared that there was going to be no need to thank her opponent.

"Odds savor of the racecourse," said the doctor.

"Quite so," said Miss Frayling innocently. "So you don't like racing, Doctor?"

"Must I answer that question?" asked the doctor.

"Well," said the judge, "I don't quite see the relevance but it doesn't seem to be a very harmful question. Why don't you like racing, Doctor?"

"It's a conspiracy," said the doctor.

"I beg your pardon," said the judge. *"What* is a conspiracy?"

"The whole thing, Your Honor," said the doctor. "It ought to be put down by the law."

Poor Mrs. Boulder could see the white flag up. He'll be off in a moment, she said to herself.

"It's the owners, trainers, jockeys and bookmakers," the doctor went on, and tried to grip the judge's arm. But Judge Hazlewell just managed to avoid the embrace. "They all conspire against you," continued the doctor. "An honest gambler hasn't a chance. They get you on the racecourse, fill you up with drink, take your money, give you a bit back to ensnare you, and then rob you right, left and center. It's a positive scandal and they're all in it together. Either the races are rigged, or the prices, or both. The whole thing's a fantastic swindle. I can prove it. The vets are in it too. Dope tests! Who takes them? Who sees the results? Every now and then they pretend to warn off a trainer or a jockey, but it's all part of the conspiracy to keep the public going. I know what I'm talking about, Your Honor. I've been there. I've been fleeced like all the others. I tell you, the judges are in it too. No offense to Your Honor. My horse won once. That, no doubt, was an accident. It had been arranged that another horse should. What happened? The judge gave the race to the other horse. They said in the press that he mistook the number. Mistook the number! The press are in it too. Look at the papers they sell. Midday editions, racing editions. Look at the tipsters. They're all laughing at you. I'm sorry, Your Honor, but it's a scandal. I repeat, it ought to be put down by the law."

"How much did you lose, Doctor?" asked Miss Frayling.

"That's not the point," said the doctor, who was now riderless and on his third circuit, the race being held up meanwhile. "I can be as sporting as the next man. If you make a gamble, you know you may lose. But you want a fair chance. That's all I ask. A fair chance. But you just don't get one."

Mrs. Boulder decided to try to catch the doctor. She stood up to ask her question.

"Dr. Crestway," she said loudly, "we're talking about Hugh West."

But the doctor ran outside her.

"The name of the horse doesn't matter," he said. "It's the principle involved."

Mrs. Boulder sat down and realized that she must wait till he slowed down from exhaustion and could be quietly captured and taken back to the paddock.

The doctor galloped on for some distance, but inevitably had to stop eventually.

"Doctor," said Miss Frayling, "I assure you that my next question is not intended to be offensive, but did you have a happy childhood?"

"Very," said the doctor, now meekly allowing himself to be led back to the stables.

"No change of home at an early age?"

"No."

"Whom d'you consult for your own troubles?"

"As a matter of fact," said Dr. Crestway, "it's Dr. Bream."

The judge knew that some psychiatrists suffered quite as badly as some of their patients, but he began to have a higher opinion of them than he had before, not so much for their learning as for their ability to preserve confidences absolutely. It must have been a great temptation to Dr. Bream to tell Randolph's advisers that he himself was treating Dr. Crestway for his little neurosis; but, until Dr. Crestway himself mentioned it, it was obvious that no one knew.

19 The Decision

THE EVIDENCE ON BOTH SIDES WAS NOW CON-
cluded and the judge adjourned the hearing until the next day.
As the parties left the Court, Jeremy took Eleanor on one side.

"Can I see you alone?" he asked.

"Of course," said Eleanor. "When?"

"Now, if I may."

"I'll tell Randolph."

She went and spoke to him and came back to Jeremy.

"Give me a cup of tea somewhere," she said.

They walked in silence to a tea shop, went in and sat down.

"I'm afraid it's about my case, not yours," said Jeremy, "that
I want to talk to you."

"I guessed as much," said Eleanor. "But how d'you think ours
is going?"

"Well, the old trick cyclists have pretty well canceled each
other out. After their performances, he can't take much notice
of either of them. You don't know how much I want you to

win. I believe I'd almost bribe the judge, if that were possible. There's nothing I wouldn't do for you."

She smiled at him.

"No one could have done more than you have. But I'm worried about Randolph. D'you think we'll win?"

"I just don't know," said Jeremy. "Some judges give you an indication of what they're thinking, but Hazlewell's been just like an oyster. Not a clue. But, if my prayers can do it, you'll win all right."

"Thank you," she said. "It's so little to say for what you've done."

"I've done nothing. It's what you've done for me. D'you know, I've had the happiest time of my life since I met you. I know you don't love me—and, in a sort of way, I don't want you to. You've had enough complications in your life already. Randolph will get his divorce soon, and I want you to live happily ever after. I'm so grateful to you for showing me what real love, the best kind of love, is. It does give me an ache sometimes, it's true, but I'm so happy to have known you, so happy to have been allowed to help you. I'm not a fool. I will fall in love with some girl someday, but I shall want something out of that love."

"I hope you get it," she said. "You'll deserve it, and she'll be very lucky."

"Oh, no, there'll be no question of deserts. Most love is like that. He wants it, she wants it, they have it. It's all very wonderful in its way, but it's not the best kind of love, like the love I have for you. I just want you to know this; and to know that if ever at any time, however long ahead it may be, I can help in any way, you'll only have to ask. Telephone me, send me a cable, call on me, anything. If I'm alive and on my feet I'll be there."

She took his hand.

"I'll always come to you," she said, "whatever happens, always to you. And now let's have a cup of tea, and talk about Dr. Bream and Dr. Crestway. Did you notice that Bream gave Crestway a lift?"

When the parties and their lawyers came before Judge Hazlewell the next day, he told them that he would like to see the child before giving a decision. "I don't think it would be a good thing for him to be brought here," he said. "So, subject to anything counsel may say, I propose that I adopt the same course as the psychiatrists. As far as seeing the child is concerned, I mean. I suggest that counsel and I go to Mr. and Mrs. Woodthorpe's this afternoon, as though we were paying an ordinary call."

Both parties agreed to the judge's suggestion, and at half-past three Mrs. Boulder, Miss Frayling and the judge arrived at the Woodthorpes' house. After they had been there a few minutes, Hugh was brought in to meet them.

"I see you have a swimming pool in your garden," the judge said to the boy.

"It's a paddle pool, really," said Hugh, "but Daddy says we'll have a proper pool when I'm older."

"D'you want to swim?" asked the judge.

"Fishes swim," said Hugh.

"Would you like to be a fish?" asked the judge.

Hugh shook his head.

"Mummy had a swimming pool in her garden when she was a little boy," he confided.

Half-an-hour later the judge and counsel left and went back to the Court. The judge offered to sit late to avoid another adjournment. First Mrs. Boulder addressed him and then Miss Frayling. They each made forcibly the points which good advocates would have been expected to make and at the end the judge gave judgment.

"This is a lamentable case," he began, "in which great distress has been caused to both parties. Most of it was, in my view, unnecessary. Having seen Mrs. West in the witness box, I am quite satisfied that, had she been brought here in the first instance and questioned about the child's parentage, she would have told the truth. Indeed, had she been pressed about the matter by the guardian or the adoption society, I fully believe that the truth would probably have emerged. In which case, although Mr. and Mrs. West might have suffered some unhappiness or even distress, it would have been nothing to what both sides have now suffered. And one side will continue to suffer. Unfortunately, in my opinion, insufficient care was taken to be sure of the position of the putative father. Often a putative father has no rights at all and would not care if he had, but that does not mean to say that care should not be taken to find out, as far as reasonably can be done, whether the putative father in each case has or has not a right to be heard on the matter. It is always possible that a mother may lie about the putative father. Normally she has no reason to do so, but it is far, far better for those concerned to take a little extra time over satisfying themselves that there is no putative father in the case with a right to be heard than to do what has happened here. If there is only one chance in a hundred thousand, why should the unnecessary risk be taken?

"The mere use of a serial number is no protection whatever to the adopters from an application to set aside the order. It is normally a protection against blackmail, but even then the information may by chance be learned by a criminal, or conceivably a mistake may be made by the Court, as in this case. I mention blackmail not because Mr. or Mrs. West are the sort of people to do anything of that kind. Subject to certain qualifications, they are people of the utmost respectability. But who was to know that they were? And, indeed, Mr. West was in jail at the time, presumed to be a criminal.

"There may be cases where an adoption order seems very desirable but where the mother, out of spite, might change her mind and withdraw her consent if pressed about the putative father. If it could be proved that she withdrew her consent out of spite, the Court could still make the adoption order, but in some cases spite might be difficult to prove. In such cases, no doubt, it would be right to weigh up the risks involved and, if the adopters preferred to risk the sudden appearance of a putative father with a right to be heard, rather than the possibility of the mother's changing her mind, not to press the mother with further questions. But in the normal case it is, in my view, quite wrong for the possibility of there being rights of a putative father to be dismissed so lightly, as they have been here. Indeed, it would have been far better for the mother to have changed her mind at a very early stage in this case, than for the present situation to have arisen.

"Now, as to the application itself, I have heard the whole of the evidence, although it is only if Mr. West can prove he is liable under an agreement to contribute to the maintenance of the child that he has any right to have the order set aside. Having heard all the evidence, I am going to give my opinion upon the case as a whole. In other words, I am going to express my view as to whether this child ought to go back to its real parents. If I or the Court of Appeal set aside the order and the application for adoption were heard again, I should have to bear in mind that the mother has now withdrawn her consent, and, unless I were satisfied that she had done so unreasonably, I could not make an adoption order, even if I thought it in the interests of the child to do so. It is perhaps strange that the legislature has leaned more in favor of a parent's rights than of a child's interests. But I have to abide by the law, and, however much an adoption order may be in the interests of a child, the order cannot be made in the absence of the mother's consent, or, if the child is legitimate, in the absence of the father's consent too, unless such consents are unreasonably refused or in a very few special cases, none of which arise here.

"Now, there is no doubt that life has been very hard on Mr. West. He has suffered, through no fault of his own, in a way for which he cannot be properly compensated. And it was during his absence in prison, when he was unable to fight for himself, that this child, to whom he is and always has been utterly devoted, was given away. It was given away because the mother lied about the child's parentage. That again was no fault of the father, but those lies, whether excusable or not, have been the main cause of this tragedy.

"One can appreciate Mrs. West's despair at the time, and I am certainly not condemning her for what she did. She made a great sacrifice to do what she thought was right. But, when one has to compare the situation of the adoptive parents—who took the child in good faith and lavished all their love and care upon it—I cannot avoid paying attention to the fact that it was the mother's lies which, however understandable, even perhaps justifiable, were the cause of the trouble. As far as the adoptive parents are concerned, no fault can be found in them of any kind. As far as the putative father is concerned, the only criticism which can validly be made is that he *is* a putative father. That is to say, that he chose to have relations with a woman out of wedlock. In such cases suffering may be caused. In most cases it is not the father who suffers, but in a rare case, such as this, where it *is* the father who suffers most, how can he legitimately complain? There is, to my mind, no question at all that, although no one could fail to feel the deepest sympathy with

Mr. West, his and Mrs. West's merits are not so great as Mr. and Mrs. Woodthorpe's.

"It would be wholly wrong of me if I tried to compensate Mr. West for his false imprisonment by giving him back the child. That is his grave misfortune, but, because he has been wronged, that is no reason for transferring the burden to wholly innocent people. So much for the merits of the parties. As to the child itself, I am bound to say that, having seen him in his present surroundings, it would have taken a great deal to persuade me that he should be taken away from them. Had it been necessary to do this, I should have done so most reluctantly and with a heavy heart. It may be that Dr. Bream is right and that he would get over the change without any ill effects. It may be that Dr. Crestway is right and that he might be injured in his personality in consequence. But the evidence of neither the one nor the other convinced me that the view of either was the right one. And I prefer to decide this case on what I have seen and heard of the parties themselves and the child, and not upon the theoretical evidence of the eminent gentlemen to whose evidence I have had the good fortune to listen.

"Looking at the matter broadly, I am quite satisfied that the child ought to remain where it is. From the purely legal point of view also, I think that Mr. West's application should fail. He was, in my view, a putative father who was *not* liable under any agreement to support the child. Had he withdrawn his support, he could have had an affiliation order made against him, but he could not have been sued under any agreement. In other words, this father never had the right to be served with the proceedings, though, of course, had the Court been aware of his existence, he certainly would have been served with them. The result is that this application fails, and the adoption order will remain. But I am sure that it was far better for me to hear the whole case and not simply to dismiss it on the technical ground that Mr. West was not liable under an agreement to support the child. Had I done so, he would always have felt that his case had never been fully heard.

"In coming to my conclusions I have, of course, borne in mind the fact that, if and when Mr. West obtains a divorce from his present wife, he and Mrs. West will marry, and that on their marriage the child will become legitimate. I accept that a divorce is likely in the near future and I feel sure that Mr. and Mrs. West will marry when a decree is granted. But legitimate children can be adopted as well as illegitimate, and, though in the normal way one would hesitate a long time before taking away their child from legitimate parents, this is by no means a normal case. I am glad to think that the child may soon be legitimized, but that fact should not, in my opinion, alter my judgment.

"There is one further matter which I think I should mention. Nothing could compensate Mr. and Mrs. Woodthorpe for the loss of this child. They cannot have children of their own and Hugh has become, as near as it is possible, a child of their own. No doubt they could adopt another child, but that would not make up for the loss of this one. The real parents, however, who, I hope, may soon be happily married, can have a further child or children and I hope that they will do so. Mr. West has shown, so far, great courage and control in adversity and I desire to express my earnest wish that for his own sake and for the sake of Mrs. West he will accept this further undeserved calamity in his life with as much philosophical restraint as is possible."

Just after the parties had left the judge's room, he sent a message to both counsel that he would like to see them. So Mrs. Boulder and Miss Frayling returned.

"Do please sit down," he said.

He did not say anything further for a short time. Eventually he said:

"Some people think that I do not approve of women at the Bar. That is quite wrong. I am delighted to see them in Court, particularly, if I may say so, when they do their work as brilliantly as both of you do."

They thanked him by a smile.

"But I must confess," he went on, "that for the first time I am a little embarrassed. In other words, I could say to you much more easily what I want to say if you were men."

"I hope you will say it just the same, Judge," said Mrs. Boulder. "If you could hear the horrible language we have to use in Court sometimes—by the way of repeating what someone else has said, I mean—it might make you less worried about it."

"It wouldn't," said the judge. "I have occasionally heard a woman member of the Bar appearing in a nuisance case, and I must confess that I'm old-fashioned enough to dislike very much hearing one of your sex say things like: 'Now, Mr. Jones, did you then say: "You ———, why don't you take your ——— to some other ———?" ' It's old age, I suppose."

"Well, if it's any consolation to you, Judge, my husband and I, who are on the best possible terms, often use what you would consider the most dreadful language to each other in the friendliest possible way. A lot of husbands and wives do."

"But—Miss Frayling . . ." the judge began.

Miss Frayling interrupted: "I'm married too, Judge," she said. "I use my maiden name for professional purposes. I am afraid I can entirely confirm what my learned colleague has said. My husband and I not only know the facts of life, but we sometimes talk about them in the crudest language to each other. Not, of course, when we can be overheard, though we've nearly slipped up about that occasionally."

"Well, it's nice of you to try to put me at my ease," said the judge. "I'm very worried about this case. Not about my decision, which, whatever Miss Frayling may think, I feel sure is right. But about your unfortunate client. I don't think he'll do anything desperate but, of course, he might. And that would be a great tragedy. But I do feel he needs immediate help. They ought to have another child as quickly as possible. And I mean as quickly as possible. Nine months from today, if that could be arranged. This may sound odd coming from me, because they're still living in adultery. But, before the child is born, they will be married, and, if West can be given this early interest of a child being on the way and then its birth, I think he will eventually be able to overcome the distress from which he is now suffering. Well now, why do I ask you? I couldn't, of course, see one of you here without the other. But it's Miss Frayling who is really concerned. Do try to get hold of your clients and persuade them of this. I know I said it in Court, but I couldn't go into details then and, coming at the end of what for them was a terrible judgment, they may hardly have heard it. Possibly you could speak to Mrs. West by herself?

"It's the urgency which I have in mind. A man in West's position might go into a fit of depression which could last for a very long time. I don't want another patient for Dr. Bream or his patient, Dr. Crestway. Please do what you can. The Woodthorpes must have suffered terribly, too, but they will be all right for the future except for the scars. But West can recover too, if only he'll move quickly. I feel sure that a man with his possessive sense will take to a new baby as he took to the first. And, once he has another baby, he can be comforted about the first because it is in good hands, could not be in better. But that comfort can never arise until he has one of his own on which to lavish all his love and hopes."

"I do so agree," said Miss Frayling. "I was even thinking of inviting the Wests and my solicitor out to dinner, filling them up with champagne, sending them home, and hoping for the best. But I hardly felt I could do it now. It would seem like a celebration."

"I am so glad," said the judge. "I can see that I'm preaching to the converted. I apologize for even indirectly suggesting that you wouldn't have thought of it yourself. It is, of course, the obvious answer. If, by any chance, you have any news in a year's time, I'd be very grateful if you'd pass it on."

"Of course, Judge," said Miss Frayling. "I'll try to get my solicitor to find out and let me know. And I'll tell you at once."

"Thank you very much," said the judge, "and thank you both for your help in this very unhappy case."

Mrs. Boulder and Miss Frayling left the judge. He sat in his chair for half-an-hour, apparently doing nothing. Suddenly, without a knock, the door opened and his clerk walked in.

"Oh—I'm so sorry," said the clerk. "I thought Your Honor had left."

"That's quite all right," said the judge, "I was just—just thinking."

He could not very well say to his clerk that he was praying for a baby for Randolph and Eleanor.

While Judge Hazlewell had been occupied in this way, Judge Bramcote was dealing with another adoption case. The applicants sat anxiously waiting for his decision.

"I gather we don't know who the putative father is," he said to their solicitor.

"That is so, Your Honor," said the solicitor.

"Well, I don't suppose he minds or cares," said Judge Bramcote. "I shall make this order with much pleasure, and I hope your clients will be very happy."

Format by Faith Nicholas
Set in Intertype Garamond
Composed and printed by York Composition Company, Inc.
Bound by The Haddon Craftsmen, Inc.
HARPER & ROW, PUBLISHERS, INCORPORATED